KU-622-690

# Warning:

*This book is about one of life's natural processes
that is an important part of health and wellbeing.*

*So ... if you don't burp,
Don't Read This Book!*

*But if belching is your thing ...
let that big bad burp sing!*

## Also by Andy Jones

*The Enormous Book of Hot Jokes for Kool Kids*
*The Fartionary*
*The Adventures of Scooterboy and Skatergirl*

# The BURP -tionary

## ANDY JONES

**Illustrated by**
**DAVID PUCKERIDGE**

ABC
Books

**ABC** Books

The ABC 'Wave' device is a trademark of the
Australian Broadcasting Corporation and is used
under licence by HarperCollins*Publishers* Australia.

First published in Australia in 2014
by HarperCollins*Children'sBooks*
a division of HarperCollins*Publishers* Australia Pty Limited
ABN 36 009 913 517
harpercollins.com.au

Text copyright © Andy Jones 2014
Internal illustrations copyright © David Puckeridge 2014

The rights of Andy Jones and David Puckeridge to be identified
as the author and illustrator of this work have been asserted by them
in accordance with the *Copyright Amendment (Moral Rights) Act 2000*.

This work is copyright. Apart from any use as permitted under the
*Copyright Act 1968*, no part may be reproduced, copied, scanned,
stored in a retrieval system, recorded, or transmitted, in any form
or by any means, without the prior written permission of the publisher.

**HarperCollins*Publishers***
Level 13, 201 Elizabeth Street, Sydney NSW 2000, Australia
Unit D1, 63 Apollo Drive, Rosedale, Auckland 0632, New Zealand
A 53, Sector 57, Noida, UP, India
77–85 Fulham Palace Road, London W6 8JB, United Kingdom
2 Bloor Street East, 20th floor, Toronto, Ontario M4W 1A8, Canada
195 Broadway, New York NY 10007, USA

National Library of Australia Cataloguing-in-Publication entry:

Jones, Andy.
The burptionary / written by Andy Jones; illustrated by David Puckeridge.
ISBN: 978 0 7333 3383 5 (paperback)
For children.
Belching–Juvenile literature.
Digestion–Juvenile literature.
Australian wit and humor–Juvenile literature.
Puckeridge, David, illustrator.
A828.302

Cover and internal design by Pigs Might Fly; adapted by Natalie Stuart
Cover illustration by Matt Stanton
Packaged by Jaclyn Crupi Professional Editorial Services
Typeset in Berkeley Oldstyle Book by Natalie Stuart
Printed and bound in Australia by Griffin Press
The papers used by HarperCollins in the manufacture of this book are
a natural, recyclable product made from wood grown in sustainable
plantation forests. The fibre source and manufacturing processes meet
recognised international environmental standards, and carry certification.

5 4 3 2 1   14 15 16 17

*To 'Bob & Peg' and their fur babies*
*and Miss Velvet my Burping Burmese.*

A. JONES

# CONTENTS

# BURPS & BELCHES IN HISTORY

# SCIENCE IN THE BOTTOM OF YOUR BELLY

# ANIMAL ERUCTATION

# THE WORLDWIDE BURP

# BURP ARTISTS

# BELCHOGA – BURPING YOGA

# BURP-SPEAK

# A BURP BY ANY OTHER NAME

# BURPY FACTS

# BURPOLOGY
## The biology of the burp

GAS! It seems like it's everywhere and everywhere it is!

Gas is in space – think of Jupiter, the giant gas planet, also known as the cosmic belch, the intergalactic burp and even the distant planet of fart!

The gas BBQ – very handy if you like flavoursome fried fritters, sizzling sausages and succulently well-done steak.

There is of course bottom gas, better known as a FART or bottom belch, fluff, frog, SBD, botty bomb, butt trumpet (see the amazing *Fartionary*, arguably the greatest testament to farting ever written).

And finally (drum roll please), tummy gas AKA burps, belches and eructations from down below in the gut where the food doth go (an homage to William Shakespeare, who many say invented the phrase 'Doth Burp').

Now let's get technical: what is a burp? The simplest definition is always the best! Simply put, a 'BURP' is an eruptive, usually smelly, loud release of GAS that has built up in your stomach and travels from your gut, exiting through your mouth.

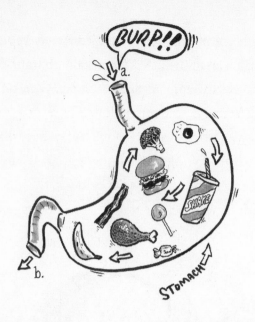

Now let's try a technical explanation – gas builds up in your stomach from gulping air and the breaking down of food by the body's release of bile acid. This is a chemical process that helps turn food into a soup-like substance that can be digested in the intestine. As the gases build up and combine with air, pressure is created. The pressure is due to the expansion of the gas in a small confined area. That gas is then expelled from the stomach through the cardiac sphincter, which is the valve that connects the stomach to the oesophagus.

Burps are mostly gas from the stomach and oesophagus as opposed to farts, which are produced by intestinal chemical processing of food. You can think of both a burp and a fart as two different types of cooking. The burp is like a bubbly fizzy smoothie in a blender – you add mineral water, banana, milk and kiwifruit and blend. You spin it out of control for a minute or so and then when you pop the lid, your ears are assaulted by a tympanic crack and out blows a gush of sound and seasoned smell.

A fart, on the other hand, is like a slow-cooked, oven-roasted, baked and basted mishmash of scents and smells (methane gas mainly) that come from many types of food. It can take days for the food to move through the intestines and be digested and chemically changed before the percussive potty blast is blown out into the world and all noses in its vicinity.

Makes you kind of hungry don't it!?!

# BURPS IN MOTION
## How burps travel through the body

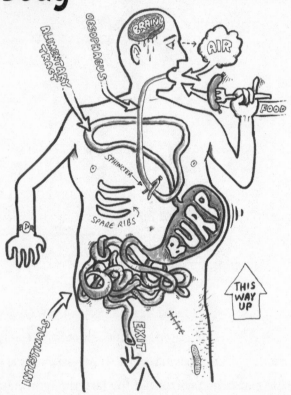

A burp, as you now know, is primarily made in your stomach and then when the gas pressure gets too high, a release valve called the cardiac sphincter opens and vents the gas to your mouth via your oesophagus, which in turn creates a burping belch blast!

6

Your sphincter opens
and closes when food
goes down from your
mouth to your stomach
but also opens and vents
gas or even vomitus into
and out of your mouth
– clever little sphincter.

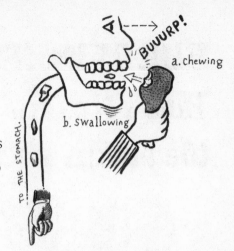

The act of swallowing
is called peristalsis; it's like squeezing a sausage from top
to bottom and squishing the food along. Peristalsis is
a natural and vital part of digestion. It starts with your
mouth making saliva when you are about to eat and
goes into overdrive with the first mouthful! As food is
swallowed so is air, which mixes with the food in your
stomach and creates a burp.

It also needs to be pointed out that some air is so single-
minded, determined and even sneaky that it gets through
the stomach and is digested with the food you have eaten.
Yes, this air becomes 'part of the fart' that you release in
the next few days.

So what is air today becomes fart tomorrow …

# THE STINKING TRUTH
## Why burps smell

Burps smell as a result of what we eat.

As we all know, any one human being can shovel down the most incredible array of food and beverages in one sitting let alone a day. So imagine having baked beans on grain bread toast for breakfast with a tomato and a poached egg. You also drink an apple juice as well as a cup of tea with it, then add a banana and maybe an orange, which just about satisfies your morning hunger or, as some people have renamed it, 'Mornger'.

Along with every bite, sip, munch, crunch, mash, swallow and chew you gulp small amounts of air. That air mixes with all of that big bad brekky that you just gobbled down, which slowly filters through your clever little sphincter into that big sloppy gruel bag known as your stomach.

Now let's think for a moment about all of that food that you have just consumed:

Baked beans
Grain bread toast
One tomato
One poached egg
Apple juice
Tea
One banana
One orange

Take all that food and drink, add about 1/4 litre of air and mix thoroughly. What do you get? You will probably get a fair to reasonable belly burp, but it will have the added bonus of the smell of the foods you have just eaten. The burp will vary in volume and force depending on how much air you gulped with the meal.

However, if you drink a fizzy or carbonated drink then you will load your gut with excess gas that will blow its way to the surface just like a volcano.

So, burps smell like a mixture of whatever you have eaten! Thank goodness no one eats smelly socks with cheese-flavoured nail clippings!!! Ewwwww …

# THE ODOROUS ORCHESTRA
## The sound of the oral woodwind section

Burps are mainly comprised of nitrogen and oxygen but if you drink fizzy drinks then the main gas component is carbon dioxide. These gases give burps the momentum to explode from the stomach up and out the mouth.

The sound, blast or belch of a burp is produced by the vibration of the gas leaving the stomach through the cardiac sphincter. The burp sounds as if it's coming from the throat but it's actually being played way down at the exit of the stomach.

# World Record - Loudest Burp

The record belongs to a belching monster from the UK named Paul Hunn. He holds the current title for burping at 109.9 decibels. This might not mean much to you but if you compare it with the decibel readings of some other machinery it will put his incredibly loud belching feat into perspective.

| | | |
|---|---|---|
| Blue Whale | 180 | DB |
| Rock Band Peak | 150 | DB |
| Thunder | 120 | DB |
| Cicadas | 120 | DB |
| Jet Take-off | 115 | DB |
| Car Horn | 110 | DB |
| Paul Hunn Burping | 109.9 | DB |
| Motorcycle | 100 | DB |
| Hand Drill | 98 | DB |
| Truck Traffic | 90 | DB |
| Normal Conversation | 60 | DB |
| Whisper in Library | 30 | DB |

# World Record - Longest Burp

This long-distance burping behemoth is from the US and his name is Tim Janus. Tim produced the longest burp, recorded at 18.1 seconds, at the World Championships! Yes, they actually have a World Championship for burps!

# THE BURP FACT FILE
## True or false?

**BF1** – The scientific name for burping is 'eructation'.

TRUE! Burping is known as ructus as well as eructation.

**BF2** – Some people cannot burp.

TRUE! Most people can burp and belch into next week but some individuals cannot burp due to two well-known medical disorders:
1. GORD (Gastric Oesophageal Reflux Disorder) which is caused by the stomach acid leaking up through the cardiac sphincter. The sphincter doesn't seal properly so gas can't build and erupt in a burp.
2. Schatzki ring, which is a smooth narrow ring of tissue that wraps around the opening of the oesophageal sphincter or stomach entrance and stops gas from coming out.

**BF3** – Boys burp more than girls.

**FALSE!** It all depends on what you eat. Both sexes burp equally.

**BF4** – You burp more in the morning.

**FALSE!** You burp whenever you swallow food, liquid or air, unlike farting, which is known all over the world as 'morning thunder' because it builds up in your intestine overnight and loves to start the day with an odorous big bang!

**BF5** – On average people burp between 6 and 15 times a day.

**TRUE!** Most people belch somewhere in that number range.

**BF6** – Famous people never burp.

FALSE! The famous burp and belch like the rest of the inhabitants of planet Earth.

**BF7** – In some cultures it is considered a compliment to the chef to burp after a meal.

TRUE! This is very true but don't try this on your mother – very bad idea!!!

**BF8** – The WBF is the worldwide organisation that sanctions all burping records.

TRUE! The WBF (World Burping Federation) with its headquarters in Geneva, Switzerland oversees decibel and duration belching competitions.

BURP·O· METER

**BF9** – The more you burp the less you fart.

TRUE! If you burp a lot then the air and gas doesn't get to your intestines and slow cook to make loud smelly butt bombs.

**BF10** – Chickens burp more than any other farm animal.

FALSE! Chickens cannot burp.

**BF11** – Astronauts in space do more wet burps than people on Earth.

TRUE! Burping in space at zero gravity affects the muscle tightening of the oesophageal sphincter, stopping it closing properly, so food can leak up and out with a big zero gravity belch.

**BF12** – Cows don't burp.

FALSE! Each year cows in the US burp about 50 million tonnes of gas into the atmosphere. If you could catch the burps of 10 cows you could keep a small house heated for 12 months.

## BF13 - All burps smell.

FALSE! This depends on what the belching beast has consumed prior to the burp. Soft drink burps often have no smell.

## BF14 - Chewing gum makes you burp more.

TRUE! As we all know, chewing gum looks cool and can give you sweet breath but you will swallow more air, which will make you burp more chewy belches.

## BF15 - An old wedding custom is to kiss the bride and then burp in her face for good luck.

FALSE! Hello!!! Are you serious? No, no and nooooo – you risk physical harm doing this.

# BURPY BELCHY GOODNESS

## After Dinner Burps

In some Asian cultures it is quite acceptable to release a loud complimentary belch after a delicious meal and is seen as a salute to the chef's cooking ability.

# Gas-guzzling Gastronomy

People can and do swallow up to 300 times per day. With each swallow they can take in 3 millilitres of air. That's a lot of big bad burp bangs.

# Underwater Burples

If you are swimming underwater and try to burp your body will have trouble due to the water pressure. It's much easier to fire off a few butt bubbles than it is to burp underwater.

# BURPY POEM

## I Like to Burp
A. JONES

Some like to slurp and some like to sup

Others love to sip and others like to suck

While some like to swig and some like to swallow

My preference is to burp and belch into tomorrow.

# BURPING
# ETIQUETTE

# BURPING NO-GO ZONES
## The dos and don'ts of the gaping gob

Even though burping is a natural part of life, there are still some dos and don'ts when it comes to this noisy, gassy bodily function.

## When not to ... (burping no-go zones!)

- **Dinner Table –** Never a good idea. However, depending on the country, a post-feast belch will either be expected or will put you behind bars.

- **Public Speaking** – When speaking in public, being in control of your presentation or speech is vital to the delivery, but sometimes an unexpected delivery arrives in the form of a big nervous belch. If possible you need to either use the belch as a vowel or swallow it just before it is released. Both methods can work well and will stop that noisy little sucker from interrupting your flow.

- **Banks** – Never let a huge belch loose in a bank because people might fear that a wild animal has gotten loose and entered the bank to make a human withdrawal.

- **Principal's Office** – Never ever ever ever (!!!) burp in the principal's direction as this will always end in tears. For you, not the principal. There will be two expulsions, your gas and you from school!

- **Weddings** – When attending a wedding never ever fire a burp off just as the celebrant asks, 'Do you take this woman to be your lawful wedded wife?' It might get a laugh but will definitely brand you as a troublemaker.

- **Dentist** – Beware of dental belches! If you belch at the dentist as he or she is looking deep into your mouth you run the risk of dental drill retribution (the dentist will try to drill new holes in your teeth).

- **Elevator** – Enclosed space belching is asking for trouble. People will think that if you belch in public you might fart in public as well.

# When to ...
# (burping safety zones!)

- **The Bath –** The bath is
your burping sanctuary.
Bubble burps are awesome.

- **Footy Game –** In fact it's almost mandatory to burp,
belch, scream and fart!
- **Party –** A party is a perfect place to share chats, stories
and of course big bad belching boo boos. Everyone
at a party is so happy that letting out a belch after
eating, chatting and drinking fizzy beverages is totally
acceptable.
- **Antarctica –** If you are lucky enough to take a trip to
Antarctica to see those funny little black-and-white
waddling birds, you will have struck burping paydirt!
Penguins make a throaty burp-like sound constantly.
In fact, if you belch as loudly and frequently as you
can in their presence you might even end up finding a
prospective marriage partner!

- **Outdoors** – Outside is a perfect place for the release and sharing of gas with mother nature.

- **Desert Island** – If you find yourself on a desert island alone with no other people, animals, food or water, then it's ok to burp to the heavens. Unfortunately this will not help you survive but you will experience almost biblical belching freedom.

# BURPY TRIVIA

- The Japanese word for burping is *geppu*. As cute as the word is, it is not considered cute to burp at the dinner table in Japan.

- Germans consider a burp after a meal of sauerkraut and sausage a compliment to the chef. In fact, it is considered rude if guests do not belch their appreciation. This idea came about from the religious reformer Martin Luther, a German priest, who was famous for saying, 'Warum furzet und rülpset ihr nicht, hat es euch nicht geschmecket?' Translated that means, 'Why don't you farteth and burpeth? Didn't you fancy the meal?' I wonder if I could introduce this to my family dinner table? Mmmmm.

# BURPING FIBS

What to say in case you let a gassy gob smacker loose.

## The Froggy Fib

'Wow, those cane toads can belt 'em out, did you hear that?'

## The Kookaburra Blow

Look up and point to the closest tree, 'Those crazy kookas!'

# The Nanna Belch

'Poor Nanna, she suffers from terrible gas!'

## The Baby Boo Boo

'Ooo, you cute little diddums. I didn't know little bubba could burp that loud.'

## Wasn't Me

Look for any poor sucker in close proximity and deny, deny, deny!

# The Backfire

'Dude, did you hear that car backfire?'

# The TV

'Did you hear that? It sounded like a dirty liquid belch.'
'Yeah man, it was on TV.'

# BURPY POEM

## I Love to Burp

A. JONES

I love to burp in the morning

I belch with all of my might

I love to burp in the evening

I belch at end of light

I love to burp in the summer

I love to belch in spring

I love to burp in autumn

But sadly

Winter's not my thing.

# BURPS & BELCHES IN HISTORY

# BURPISTORY
## Burps in history

## What do ...

Julius Caesar, Winston Churchill, Neil Armstrong, Beyoncé, One Direction, J.K. Rowling, Amelia Earhart, Oprah Winfrey, Salvador Dali, General Gluteus Maximus Magnifico and even SpongeBob have in common? The answer is all of these talented individuals have created history by doing amazing things ...

# AND ...

all of them have risen to the challenge and expelled gassy gut blasts into the air! Famous writers, musicians, painters and sculptors have all paid homage to the BURP!

## William Shakespeare

Did you know that William Shakespeare created a character who belches in the play, *Twelfth Night*? He is actually required to belch and burp in the play whilst delivering lines such as, 'There's some gentlemen out there (belching), damn these pickled herring, they upset my stomach.'

# Harry Potter

'BELCH' powder was a product sold in relation to the
Harry Potter movies and books. It apparently caused the
user or victim to burp and belch uncontrollably. I wonder
if a teacher could taste it in his or her morning coffee???

# The Simpsons

Every Simpsons cartoon watcher would be used to the
belches of Bernard (Barney) Arnold Gumble. Barney
belches in every show at every opportunity and has
taken burping to a higher level by using it as a form
of communication and guttural language, hail Barney
Brrrrrrrrrrrrp!

# BURPING IN THE ANCIENT WORLD
## A big belch in history

Myth or legend? It depends who you believe. The
story goes that in about 160 AD, a huge Roman army
of roughly 10,800 soldiers camped at the foothills of
a giant forest in northern Bavaria which was home to
15,000 Germaniacs who were from nine different tribes:
The Buttoxen, The Bumhousen, The Cheekeeyou, The
Fartoulisch, The Bumf, The Fizzerlicht, The Kracken,
The Booboo-bang and the Tailtrumpetzon. These nine
tribes had united under the command of 'Anusminus of
the Kracken' to resist the Roman legions and drive them
south.

On the day of the first battle, the Germaniacs had
amassed in a one-kilometre straight line facing the
10,800-strong Roman infantry. There was a distance of
roughly 800 metres between the two armies. The Roman
general, Gluteus Maximus Magnificus, sent a message
via a Roman screamer. The screamer rode on horseback
to a point exactly halfway between the two armies and

turned to
the Germaniacs
and screamed, 'All
Germaniacs, the Great Gluteus
Maximus Magnificus is willing on
this great day to make you all full
Roman citizens if you surrender and
hail to the Roman empire. If you do, this
day will be celebrated with a huge feast.'

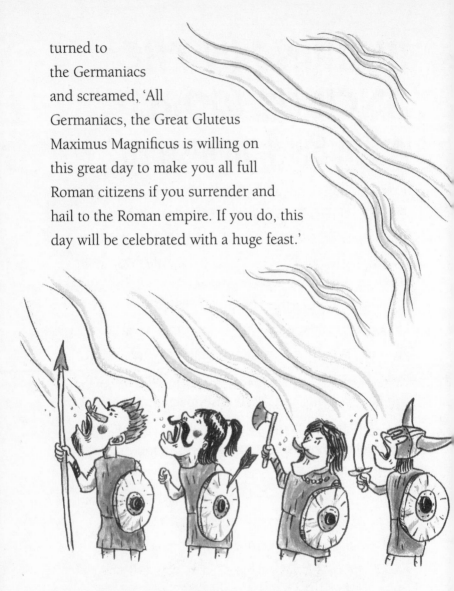

Silence gripped the Germaniacs, they looked at each
other and mumbled quietly until their leader Anusminus
walked out in front of his army and threw his hands
in the air. He screamed at the Romans, 'Mighty Rome

can feast on the rancid smell of rotten meat!' In an orchestrated move, he dropped his arms by his sides and at that very moment every Germaniac soldier leaned his head back, opened his mouth as wide as it would go and released the biggest, loudest, most guttural explosive mass burping belch directly at the Romans. It is reputed to have been so loud it made the ground rumble for a good 18 seconds, which as it happens is just short of the current belching world record. The Romans were slowly covered in a thick gaseous cloud of rancid-smelling meat that made many want to puke on the spot. Projectile vomit hurled in every direction.

This is the first time in history a belch was used as a weapon in war. The Roman general Gluteus Maximus Magnificus was so disgusted and disturbed by the incredible stench of the massive Germanic belch that he decided to call off the invasion and go home. So the message here is the beefy belch is mightier than the sword.

# BURPY TRIVIA

- Did you know that the Sun burps? Scientists have named this curious phenomenon the Sun burp, which is a solar eruption that involves plasma writhing off the surface of the sun. These eruptions or solar flares can often send solar material to Earth and beyond.

- Huge belches of methane gas from bogs in the UK are now being blamed as a contributing factor to global warming. The methane mass, which scientists are suggesting was belched from these bogs 55 million years ago, could have heated the arctic waters to 23 degrees Celsius.

# BURPY POEM

## Pardon Me

ANONYMOUS

*Pardon me for being so rude.*
*It was not me, it was my food.*
*It got so lonely down below,*
*It just popped up to say hello.*

# SCIENCE
## IN THE
# BOTTOM
### OF YOUR
# BELLY

# BURPING BLISS
## The blessed release of the belch

Like many bodily functions, when something is released the body usually responds with a feeling of relief. This is what that relief might sound like:

Pee pee (micturition) – aaaaaaah

Doing a poo (defecation) – plop plop plop aaaah

Vomit (emesis) – blahhhhhhhhh aaaaaaah

Fart (flatus or flatulence) – oh yeah

Burp (eructation) – eeeeeehhhh

Here are some words related to these bodily functions:

Pee – Splish, Splash, Dribble, Spray, Squirt, Swoosh, Tinkle

Poo – Plip, Plop, Flap, Flop, Plap, Plonk

Vomit – Slosh, Splosh, Sputter, Splutter, Slop, Glop

Fart – Bang, Pop, Blast, Honk, Toot, Bloomp

Burping is said to be one of the most satisfying feelings that the human body can produce. This is primarily due to the build up and release of gut gas.

So in theory, your stomach is like a balloon full of air, well, a pear-shaped pink balloon with a yellowish tinge – a balloon that has a gastric soup of hydrochloric acid and protein digestive enzymes floating at the base of it. This gut balloon plays a role in the digestion process but most digestion takes place in the small intestine.

Your pink gut balloon takes in the food and churns and breaks it into smaller particles called 'chyme'. Many people think that you digest the food you eat in the order that you swallow it but this is not true because your pink gut balloon with a yellow tinge is also like a washing machine! Yes, it's a top-loading, single spin cycle, green bile-infused agitation machine.

Here is a sample menu from YOUR birthday dinner:
Entrée – Garlic prawns and sourdough bread
Main – Roast lamb (Nanna style), potatoes, pumpkin, onions and steamed broccoli and Brussels sprouts all served with gravy

Dessert – Apple pie with ice-cream and cream
EXTRAS – Add two or three glasses of fizzy drink and
some sweets (for colour)

Now imagine tipping all
of that food into a
strong plastic bag,
sealing it and shaking
it up really well – I
mean flinging the
bag around your
head in the air and
shaking it side to
side and up and
down … and then
pause. Now imagine
looking at the bag
– you would see
a multi-coloured
kaleidoscope

of gelatinous soft squishy goopy slop that looks like
a compost bin. This, my friends, is exactly what your
stomach does to all that floats, slides and slithers down
your throat into that big pink- and yellow-tinged balloon-
like sack before it squishes through your oesophageal
sphincter from your tummy into the small intestine to start
digestion.

# BURP CHARTS
## Graph for the gas

It's time to take your first step in becoming a burpologist. You can use these two graphs to record and log all of your research data. This will help you ascertain your burp and belch status, so I bid you gassy good luck!

The Burp Chart and Food Chart will tell you …

- The number of times you burp per day

- The number of times you burp per week

- The type of burps you do and how loud and long they are

- The time of the day (morning, afternoon, night) when you burp the most

- The types of foods that might increase burping

You will need a notepad and pen to collect the information each day and then you can add it to your Burp Chart and Food Chart each night.

# Food Chart

**Step 1:** Look at the sample Food Chart on pages 52–53. You can either draw up your own Food Chart (using felt-tip pens and a piece of cardboard), or photocopy the blank Food Chart from pages 56–57. Stick your Food Chart somewhere you will see it every day. (For example, on your wardrobe door!)

**Step 2:** Each day, write down everything you eat on the Food Chart (and I mean absolutely everything!). Every little bit of food you eat (including morning tea, afternoon tea and snacks) has to be written down to make sure it's accurate. (Remember, we are searching for the scientific truth here!) That means every sandwich, biscuit, lolly, banana, muesli bar and piece of chewing gum has to be recorded. Then you will be able to study the information you have collected at the end of the week.

# Burp Chart

**Step 1:** Look at the sample Burp Chart on pages 54–55. You can either make your own Burp Chart (using felt-tip pens and a piece of cardboard), or photocopy the blank Burp Chart from pages 58–59. Keep your Burp Chart near your Food Chart!

**Step 2:** Each day you must log every belch, burp and even squeak that comes from your mouth. For extra detail you could include the duration of each burp and the volume level. You must also record what type of burp or belch it was (see key below).

# Burp Key

| | |
|---|---|
| **NB** | Normal Burp (1–2 seconds) |
| **BA** | Baaaaaaaarp, sounds exactly like that with the emphasis on the 'Ba' (2–5 seconds) |
| **BBB** | Big Bad Belch, full sounding, guttural, loud, low open-throated belch |
| **PSB** | Pitch Shift Burp, the pitch can go from low to high or change as it is blown out |
| **SC** | Short Croak, like a frog croak but short |
| **MC** | Multi Croak, multiple rapid-fire burps |
| **MB** | Mutant Belches, any burp that doesn't fit into another category |
| **BB** | Bubble Burp, feels like it comes up in an air bubble |
| **WB** | Wet Burp, comes out as a sloppy belch (carrots included) |

# SAMPLE FOOD CHART

| Monday | Tuesday | Wednesday | Thursday |
|--------|---------|-----------|----------|
| **Breakfast**<br>• 2 boiled eggs with toast soldiers, orange juice, glass of Milo<br>• Muesli bar, 4 caramel buds | **Breakfast**<br>• 2 Weetbix with banana and milk, orange juice, toast with baked beans<br>• 2 cheese sticks | **Breakfast** | **Breakfast** |
| **Lunch**<br>• Ham and cheese sandwich, apple juice, chocolate cupcake<br>• Grilled cheese on toast, pineapple juice | **Lunch**<br>• Chicken, lettuce and mayonnaise sandwich, orange juice, fruit sticks<br>• Milo | **Lunch** | **Lunch** |
| **Dinner**<br>• Chicken schnitzel, mashed potatoes and beans, ice-cream with peaches<br>• Hot chocolate | **Dinner**<br>• Lentil soup, sausages with fried onions and cabbage, stewed apples and prunes with ice-cream | **Dinner** | **Dinner** |

| Friday | Saturday | Sunday |
|--------|----------|--------|
| Breakfast | Breakfast | Breakfast |
| Lunch | Lunch | Lunch |
| Dinner | Dinner | Dinner |

# SAMPLE BURP CHART

| Monday | Tuesday | Wednesday | Thursday |
|--------|---------|-----------|----------|
| **Breakfast** | **Breakfast** | **Breakfast** | **Breakfast** |
| NB  NB  MC  SC  WB | PSB  SC  BBB | | |
| **Lunch** | **Lunch** | **Lunch** | **Lunch** |
| RA  PSB | MC  WB  BBB | | |
| **Dinner** | **Dinner** | **Dinner** | **Dinner** |
| PSB  MB | NB  NB  PSB  SC | | |

| Friday | Saturday | Sunday |
|--------|----------|--------|
| Breakfast | Breakfast | Breakfast |
| Lunch | Lunch | Lunch |
| Dinner | Dinner | Dinner |

## Burp Key

**NB** Normal Burp (1–2 seconds)

**BA** Baaaaaaaarp, sounds exactly like that with the emphasis on the 'Ba' (2–5 seconds)

**BBB** Big Bad Belch, full sounding, guttural, loud, low open throated belch

**PSB** Pitch Shift Burp, the pitch can go from low to high or change as it is blown out

**SC** Short Croak, like a frog croak but short

**MC** Multi Croak, multiple rapid-fire burps

**MB** Mutant Belches, any burp that doesn't fit into another category

**BB** Bubble Burp, feels like it comes up in an air bubble

**WB** Wet Burp, comes out as a sloppy belch (carrots included)

# FOOD CHART (for photocopying)

| Monday | Tuesday | Wednesday | Thursday |
|---|---|---|---|
| Breakfast | Breakfast | Breakfast | Breakfast |
| Lunch | Lunch | Lunch | Lunch |
| Dinner | Dinner | Dinner | Dinner |

| Friday | Saturday | Sunday |
|---|---|---|
| Breakfast | Breakfast | Breakfast |
| Lunch | Lunch | Lunch |
| Dinner | Dinner | Dinner |

# BURP CHART (for photocopying)

| Monday | Tuesday | Wednesday | Thursday |
|--------|---------|-----------|----------|
| Breakfast | Breakfast | Breakfast | Breakfast |
| Lunch | Lunch | Lunch | Lunch |
| Dinner | Dinner | Dinner | Dinner |

| Friday | Saturday | Sunday |
|--------|----------|--------|
| Breakfast | Breakfast | Breakfast |
| Lunch | Lunch | Lunch |
| Dinner | Dinner | Dinner |

# GURGLE BURGLES

A 'Gurgle Burgle' is a term that refers to babies. Babies cannot burp and belch like adults because they can't move around freely which makes it very difficult for them to burp. Babies also swallow large amounts of air when they suck a dummy, bottle or even their thumb. This air pools in their small stomach. This can be a problem because their lack of movement traps the air inside their stomach. It then filters into their intestine, swells and backs up, causing colic pain.

Colic is very uncomfortable for a baby and that is why parents are encouraged to BURP their babies manually.

A Gurgle Burgle is the sound a baby makes when it is manually burped. This sometimes produces milk and fluid to be secreted with the BURP! Yesssssss it's starting to sound a little like projectile vomit, isn't it?

# REDUCING RUCTUS
## Ways to reduce belching

As fun as burping is, if you want to reduce your ructus ruckus there are some things you can do.

- Don't drink too many fizzy or carbonated soft drinks.
- Don't shovel food down quickly; you swallow extra air with your glutinous gulping.
- Chew with your mouth closed, also good to stop flies landing in your gob.

- Don't chew gum for long periods of time as it makes you swallow more air and look like a cow!
- Don't eat too much food in one sitting, the more you chow down the more you gas up.
- Sip drinks slowly and don't use a straw because you get as much air as fluid.
- Sucking candies and lollies can also make you burp due to the air intake.
- Drinking herbal tea can reduce belching, so sup some nice cha.

# BURP BUBBLES
## H₂O belches

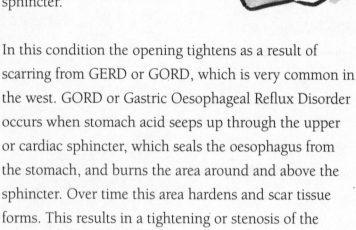

Some people say that they
feel as if they are burping
small bubbles. This can be
due to a medical condition
known as stenosis. Stenosis is
a narrowing of the oesophageal
sphincter.

In this condition the opening tightens as a result of
scarring from GERD or GORD, which is very common in
the west. GORD or Gastric Oesophageal Reflux Disorder
occurs when stomach acid seeps up through the upper
or cardiac sphincter, which seals the oesophagus from
the stomach, and burns the area around and above the
sphincter. Over time this area hardens and scar tissue
forms. This results in a tightening or stenosis of the
oesophagus.

Burp bubbles can occur when saliva mixes with air from
swallowing and this mixture gets stuck above the stenosis
and comes back up to the throat, thus making you feel
little burp bubbles are popping in your throat.

# Burpin' belch experiments (BBEs)

**BBE #1:** This is an experiment to do on your own. Get a bottle or can of your favourite carbonated soft drink. Open it and take one small gulp then wait, then take two gulps and then wait. It usually takes about three gulps before you are rewarded with a blast of gut gas.

**BBE #2:** You can do this experiment on your own as well. Drink three to six gulps of soft drink and try to hold all the gas down as long as you can – the longer the better. After you have waited for roughly five minutes stand up straight and lean backwards, then place your hands on your hips and push your stomach muscles down and tilt your head back – this should squeeze the gas into a sharp loud belch blast that will feel super satisfying!

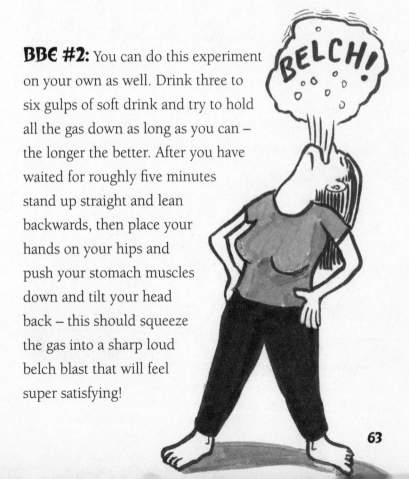

**BBE #3:** You can do this one alone or with a friend. The trick is to gulp a whole can or small bottle of soft drink completely, holding the urge to burp! You need to then bend and stretch like you are warming up for sport. Touch your toes, crouch down, squat but you must hold onto that belching urge at all times. When you feel that you are going to explode, let it out and time your belch.

| | |
|---|---|
| 2–5 seconds | Average |
| 5–8 seconds | Pretty Tidy |
| 8–10 seconds | Epic |
| 10–12 seconds | Gas Master Status |
| 12–14 seconds | Gas Master 1st Dan Status |
| 14–18 seconds | Total BEAST – You are an ANIMAL |
| 18+ seconds | NEW WORLD RECORD! |

**BBE #4:** This is perfect for parties and can be enjoyed by both boys and girls in groups. Get all the gassy party animals to sit in a circle. Each person must have a can or bottle of carbonated soft drink in front of them on the ground. You need a timekeeper to time these fizzy party feats of gaseousness. Going in a clockwise direction, one by one each person takes a gulp of their fizzy drink and then prepares and when ready belts out a belch, which is timed. The longest belch wins! Also each person only has 15 seconds to prepare the burp. Happy belching you pack of animals.

**BBE #5:** The idea of this experiment is to see if you can burp while upside down. You need to take off your shoes and have the use of a wall that you are allowed to do a handstand against. You can get a friend to hold your legs in the air as you do a handstand against the wall. But before you do the handstand, you need to have a gulp of a fizzy drink. Once upside down, try to burp.

**BBE #6:** The idea of this experiment is to try and identify what you can smell in your burp. Lift a glass or cup to your mouth and burp into it. Quickly cover the top of the glass or cup with your hand, wait about one minute until your nose is clear, then slowly slip your nose into the glass but keep it sealed. Try to identify the smells.

**BBE #7:** For this experiment you need to see if you can change the pitch of your burp. Take a big gulp of a can or bottle of fizzy drink and hold it, then try to burp. As the burp comes out you need to see if you can change the pitch, that is, make the burp sound higher or lower. It's actually quite hard to do so if you can do this you are becoming the burpologist I knew you had inside you!

# BURP TRIVIA

- Did you know that billions of tiny bacteria live in your intestines to help digestion? They turn some of the undigested food into vitamin K and vitamin B or chyme, which makes its way into your small intestine to start being digested.

- Did you know that your stomach coats itself in a protective mucous membrane-like substance? This coating stops the stomach acid from burning your gut lining and eating itself.

- Did you know that a newly discovered stomach bacteria called *deinococcus radiodurans* is one of the hardiest organisms alive? Radiodurans is a so-called extremophile because it thrives in extreme environments that would kill most organisms, such as radioactive waste dumps and hot springs. It can survive heat, cold, vacuum and acid. It is so resilient scientists nicknamed it 'Conan the Bacterium' after the fictional barbarian warrior.

# BURPY POEM

## A Burp

A. JONES

Little bubbles in your mouth,
Gassy visitors from down south
They fizz and foam and froth and bubble
When released are always trouble
Some explode with barking bang
Others croak with toad-like twang
Scent of flowers is never present
Rotten food is effervescent
Belching loudly can be alarming
Only babies make it charming
They say girls burp with delicate pitch
Men belch loudly like scratching an itch
Pop burps a lot, though it's hard to know
The origin of the blast, sounds from below
You would be lucky to hear royalty burp
Though I'm quite convinced that royalty slurp
Burps can be wet, belches can be dry
Both can be born when you cry
A belch is not a hiccup, no relation at all
A burp is your tummy trying to climb over the wall.

# ANIMAL
# ERUCTATION

# WHICH ANIMALS DO AND WHICH ANIMALS DON'T!
## Belching in the wild kingdom

That fantastic, amazing, unbelievable, fact-packed, portable encyclopedia of all things farty *The Fartionary* tells us that you need guts, or more specifically intestines, to manufacture and produce flatulence (farts). So if an animal doesn't have intestines, it won't fart. Not all animals have the guts to produce flatulence, and this is the same for eructation or burping.

Now I can tell you this, primates such as monkeys have a stomach, small intestine and a large intestine or bowel. This enables them to manufacture flatulence. I can hear you ask yourself, are humans primates? Well the short answer is YES! Believe it or not, human beings are just another primate from the African continent.

Humans adapted and evolved to the point where our thumbs became opposable, which means they can be used for grasping. This is a very useful adaptation if you like to pick things up. We have created new and unusual uses for our opposable thumbs such as the nose pick, rolling boogies between our thumb and finger and squeezing big fat juicy pus-filled pimples on our faces.

# THE ANIMAL KINGDOM'S GASEOUS GUT LAUNCHERS

## Cow

Cows expel gas which is mainly methane. Methane is produced as a by-product of digestion. The average cow can belch between 200 and 300 litres of methane per day, which is thought to have a significant effect on global warming.

# Sheep

Sheep are also cud chewers like cows. They can belch up to 100 litres of methane per day.

# Deer

Deer produce their fair share of methane gas, but their numbers are not as high as cows, sheep and goats.

# Goat

The 'Belching Goat' sadly is not the name of a Middle Eastern restaurant. Goats are also cud-chewing ruminants. They produce lots of methane gas, though not as much as cows and sheep, but they are in the top five methane-making machines.

# Human

We burp up to 15 times a day. Humans burp and belch like no other animal on Earth. This is mostly due to our digestive system, which has a mouth, throat, oesophagus, intestines and stomach and runs in an almost straight line punctuated with sphincters that open and close to let food in and gas out and vice versa.

Humans eat a massive range of food compared to animals in the wild, who are limited by what is available. Add to that carbonated drinks and the fact that we gulp lots of air when eating and you can understand humans being up in the Top 5 burping species on the planet! You can also put us in the Top 5 farting species, Top 5 sleeping species and Top 5 skin-shedding species, but that's another book!

# Monkey

These guys burp up to 100 times per day. Monkey burps are usually a little wet. They often smell like banana.

# Dog

Yes, pooches can and do burp. Dog burps are mostly caused by eating or drinking too quickly and they can be very smelly depending on what the dog is being fed – liver treat-smelling burp, ewwww!

# Kangaroo

Kangaroos are now known as the 'Green Ticked' planet-friendly grass eaters because scientists have discovered that their burps have much less methane gas than their grass-eating cousins, cows, sheep and goats.

# Camel

Camels are also card-carrying members of the ruminant family, even though they look more like a moose on the loose. They are likely to spit at you after they belch!

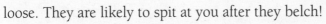

# ANIMALS THAT JUST CAN'T BELCH

## Rat

Rats do not belch, burp or vomit. They have evolved without the muscle and neurological connections that fire the process of vomiting. A rat has a few strategies to prevent needing to vomit. It will only eat a very small amount of a new food and if it feels nauseous it will not eat that food again. If it starts to feel really sick it will eat clay, which is really good at binding to the toxin and neutralising its toxicity, before pooing it out.

## Chicken

Most people think that chickens cannot burp, but many experts agree that it could be possible for birds to burp because they can regurgitate food to feed their young. The majority of people say that they have never heard of a chicken burping!

# Cat

The kitty jury is out! Vets and cat owners cannot agree
about whether cats burp. Some people say they hear their
cat burp but it is usually just before it brings up a fur-ball!
Many vets say that cats do not burp, the burping gurgling
sound cat owners hear is not a burp, but a pre-gurgle
fur-ball regurgitation.

# GAS-GULPING EMERGENCIES

## Gastroparesis – This is a medical condition that can to lead to excessive belching. It is characterised by food sitting in the stomach longer than it should due to sluggish and weak tummy muscles. Food is unable to be pushed out of the stomach to be digested.

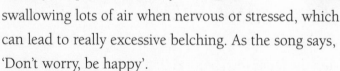

## GORD – Also known as gastric reflux, GORD can cause excessive belching and be very uncomfortable.

## Anxiety Burps –

Anxiety burps are caused by swallowing lots of air when nervous or stressed, which can lead to really excessive belching. As the song says, 'Don't worry, be happy'.

## Fizzy Wizzy Overdose – We have all been there, too much carbonated drink which means bloat, burp and belch are all on the way.

# THE BURPING BOVINE AND FRIENDS

Methane derives largely from the digestive processes of cattle and sheep and is mostly due to burping as the cud is re-chewed. Methane also comes from manure.

Cows must chew their food twice to digest it properly, spending up to nine hours and 40,000 jaw movements per day.

A cow's first bite or mouthful is chewed just enough to moisten the food, then it is swallowed and makes its way to the first section of its digestive system, the rumen. The rumen is where the food is mixed with other acidic digestive liquids and is softened into small balls of food called cud.

The rumen muscles regurgitate the cud back up to the cow's mouth, it is re-chewed and swallowed a second time and is sent to the omasum section of stomach, which squeezes all of the moisture out.

Finally, the food enters the abomasum in the stomach where it mixes with digestive juices and moves into the intestines to be completely digested.

If cows and other ruminants do not belch they can become very sick and develop bloat, which is methane gas building up in the intestines and expanding. If the pressure builds up to an excessive level it can rupture, tearing the intestine, which can be fatal for the animal.

# BURP AND BELCH FUNNIES

**Q:** What colour is a burp?
**A:** *Burp-le.*

**Q:** What did one burp say to the other?
**A:** *Let's be stinkers and play on through to the other end.*

**Q:** Why didn't the skeleton burp?
**A:** *He didn't have the guts.*

A man belched a massive burp and a man nearby said, 'How dare you burp before my wife!'
*The burper replied, 'I didn't realise she wanted to go first.'*

**Q:** What's the difference between a fart and a burp?
**A:** *You fart and you waste – you burp and you taste.*

**Q:** What happened to the boy who drank 8 cans of fizzy lemonade?
**A:** *He burped 7 Up.*

# RUMINANTS VS HUMANS

| Ruminant | Human |
|---|---|
| Burps and belches up to 200 times per day. | Burps and belches 15 to 20 times per day. |
| Farts 50 plus times per day. | Farts 15 to 30 times a day on average. |
| Eats grass, chews grass, swallows grass, grass is processed into small balls called cud, regurgitates the grass, chews again and swallows. | Eats everything, semi chews everything, eats more, swallows everything, feels bloated, moves around and belches. |
| Is good to eat. | Not good to eat, tastes like chicken. |
| Can turn grass into milk. | Cannot turn grass into milk. |
| Never breaks the law or commits a crime. | Breaks the law and commits crimes. |
| Never fights or is violent, flees from trouble. | Fights physically and verbally. |
| Cannot drive a car. | Can drive a car, sometimes quite badly! |
| Cannot pick its nose, cannot get its hoof to its nose. | Can pick, will pick and sometimes will even eat it. |
| Can mow your lawn with its mouth. | Cannot mow lawn with its mouth, only with a lawnmower. |
| Cannot fly a plane. | Can fly a plane. |

# BURPING TRIVIA

Here are some burpy facts that you might not already know.

- Scientists at the Commonwealth Scientific and Industrial Research Organisation (CSIRO) in Perth, Australia have developed an anti-methanogen vaccine to minimise the methane content in cow burps.

- New Zealand has 45 million sheep, nearly 10 times the human population, as well as 10 million cows, 1 million farmed deer and an unknown number of goats.

- In Palmerston North, New Zealand, an organisation called the Pastoral Greenhouse Gas Research Consortium is home to 10 'respiration chambers', which scientists use to measure the burps and belches of sheep.

- A mature dairy cow can produce more than 45.3 kilos of manure a day!

# BELCH
# 'N'
# PHYSICS

# BELCH 'N' PHYSICS

Belching as it relates to physics is a simple affair. Gas builds up in your stomach and the pressure becomes so extreme that if you do not burp, you will explode and die!

As I mentioned earlier, your stomach is very similar to a pink pear-shaped balloon. If the balloon pressure becomes too great, the balloon continues to expand and eventually it bursts.

Burping is a normal bodily function that is a relief valve for excess gut gas, so you might as well enjoy the welling, climbing sensation of the gas and of course the 'burplosion' at the end!

## ISAAC NEWTON

A funky physicist who created the laws of motion, Newton was a very intelligent man who spent more time fussing with physics than doing his hair. So he did have many bad hair days, but he also had many fantastic days with amazing physics discoveries.

Newton told us that if an object is not moving, it will not move by itself, unless it is compelled to change its state by the action of an external force. This is what is commonly known as inertia.

So Newton's bad hair stayed as it was because there was a lack of motion.

**Hair x No Brushing or Combing – External Force = BAD HAIR**

# Burpinertia

If the gut gas builds up to bursting point in a confined space like your pink pear-shaped gut balloon, expanding gas pressure is the external force that blows your goo goo gas out like a volcano. This is what is commonly known as the law of inertia (burpinertia).

## May the Force be with You

Newton's second law of motion states that the acceleration of an object produced by the applied force is directly related to the magnitude of the force. Sounds complicated but it's not. In relation to burping, the higher the pressure and the more force with which the belch is released, the faster it will travel. But the speed of the burp is also affected by the volume (amount) of the gas. If the burp is made of lots of gas, its explosion will be longer due to the larger volume of gas. If the burp is a little squeaker it will be a short burp due to the smaller volume of gas.

Apparently whilst sitting under an apple tree relaxing, Newton's noggin was hit by a falling apple. This led to him formulating his law of gravity. The burp that followed his noggin nudge inspired his famous laws of motion: the law of inertia, the law of velocity and the law of reaction. Yes, Mr Newton, you had it going on!

NOTE – This is pretty much true and every effort has been made to 'interp-burp-pret' Newton's laws. Whilst most of the facts in this book are 100% accurate, creative licence has been used to directly relate Isaac Newton's laws to burping.

# CARBONATED CULINARY CUISINE

# ESSENTIAL CREDENTIALS
## How to create bigger better badder belches

There are a few physical things that you can do to create bigger better badder belches. Your posture is very important if you want to burp on demand. Sitting down definitely helps with burp production and launch. If you sit down and lean back, almost pushing your stomach into the air, it helps create some serious burpage. It's all about the pressure exerted on your stomach and also that your oesophagus has a straight run to your mouth.

- **The Fizzy Guzzle** – Drink a fizzy soft drink, sparkling juice or mineral water as quickly as you can. This is guaranteed to make your belly blast like the best of them. This is pure 100% belch jet fuel!

BRRRUPPP

- **The Homer Belly Flop** – Posture, posture, posture! Great belching is always aided by correct posture. Like Homer Simpson, you need to sit back and do the Homer Belly Flop. Let it all hang out ... Ahhh, now that's better isn't it?

- **The Gob Gorge** – Eating food really quickly is also a sure fire way to get your burp groove on! When you shovel lots of food down quickly you gulp and swallow copious quantities of air, which creates the perfect formula for some serious gas explosions.

- **The Statue of Liberty Burp** – This great landmark stands straight and tall with a regal air of patriotism and confidence and that is exactly how you can achieve an amazing burp. You need to stand up as straight as you can, then place your right hand where your stomach meets your chest. Now press gently and quickly swallow five gulps of air. Hold it in for a few seconds and then tilt your head back and look up to the sky and press, squeeze and belt one out.

# THE SEVEN DEADLY BELCHY STINKERS

- **The Cola Belch** – Most cola drinks have a smell that has been described as, 'sickly sweet vinegar acid' – hmmm never thought of it quite that way. Because cola is soooooo sweet and so super carbonated it can produce some of the stinkiest belches ever. Save this little beasty of a burp for your brothers and sisters.

- **The Garlic Gush** – Garlic is used in many cuisines and has an unmistakable taste which lifts the flavour value in every dish it's found in. It also has the most rank, harsh and almost human sweat-like smell while being digested. Garlic breath on the day of consumption is very harsh but the next day it is positively toxic. CAUTION – If you can summon a garlic belch and deliver it at close range you will destroy all who stand before you, the only survivors will be others who ate garlic as well.

- **The Milkshake Burp** – This sneaky little dairy delicacy can pack quite a pungent burp. Milk can ferment in the stomach rather quickly and when mixed with swallowed air can produce a rather smelly rotten milk odour. If you consumed the milk on a very hot day then this will definitely make the milk ferment even more quickly. The milkshake burp is great to use on school friends after you all guzzle chocolate milk at lunch.

- **The Warm Morning Gush** – Ewwwww, this is a pungent and rotten species of burp. Everyone can lay claim to these AM fruity belchies which arrive almost like Swiss railway clockwork. Never ever fire one off in your mum's direction as she will make you gargle, floss and brush your teeth again.

- **The Wet Onion** – These special sloppy gut blasts are usually accompanied by a little amount of moisture, which adds to the eye-watering onion smell. The wet onion can be belched at close range but also from one metre away with devastating effect.

- **The Cabbage Pop** – Put simply, cabbage smells. It smells cooked or raw and when eaten and even partly digested it can really stink up a house. Digested cabbage that is passed as wind is one of the smelliest stinkiest odours that the human sense of smell can process. Cabbage consumed will be 60% broken down in the stomach in one hour. Now you have access to one of the smelliest burp weapons available. A cabbage pop can have quite an odour bouquet – rotten egg, faeces, rotten vegetables and sweaty feet.

- **The Poo (Faeces) Breath Belch** – This is the scariest, smelliest, most yuck burp of all. Unfortunately some people suffer from halitosis (bad breath) and the extreme form is having breath that smells like faeces – poo. Some other people can produce a poo-smelling belch, which is the most offensive burp of all. If people tell you that your burps smell like faeces or you smell it yourself then you should go to a doctor. If you fire off a poo belch only use it at your sworn enemies or opposing football teams.

# SEVEN GASSY MASSY DASTARDLY DEADLY DISHES
## Burp fuel

### Cola, Ice-Cream, Sausage Roll & Bread

This mix sounds weird
but is a holiday staple for
kids out and about at festivals,
fetes, parties, cinemas, beaches
or even shopping centres. It's a very
powerful mix of sweet sugars, milk, bread
and meat. Swallow, shake, churn and belch baby!

## Tomatoes and Onions

Cooked together, tomatoes and onions will age like a fine
smelly gassy wine in your guts. You can expect quite loud
and low belching blows.

# Baked Beans

Beans on toast never fails to produce gas and flatulence (burps and farts). It works each time, every time!

# Cabbage and Sausage

German-style Kransky and sauerkraut (sausage and cabbage) breaks down quickly in the stomach because of the high water content. It starts to ferment and get smelly with the decomposing sausage in your gut and will deliver belching gold within 30 minutes.

# Tomato Soup

Tomatoes become rotten quicker than any other fruit or vegetable. Slurping soup makes you swallow more air, which makes you burp more – add tomatoes and you have a lovely belchy broth with the added burp power of semi-rotten tomatoes.

## Eggs & Eggs

Eggs seem to smell as soon as you cook them, whether they're fried, poached, boiled or scrambled. If you eat eggs you will get an eggy methane gassy belch burping dividend (win). Eggstra-odinary!

## Garlic Prawns

There is nothing like the excitement of watching a bowl of sizzling hot garlic prawns being placed in front of you ready to devour. Garlic and prawns make the burp fuel of champions!

# GASSY FUNNIES

**Q:** What do you call a burp that you sit on?
**A:** *A fart.*

**Q:** What type of burps do Welsh people do?
**A:** *They belsh.*

**Q:** What is invisible and smells like milk and biscuits?
**A:** *Santa's burps.*

**Q:** Did you hear the joke about the burp?
**A:** *You wouldn't want to. It stinks!*

Knock Knock.
Who's there?
Burp.
Burp who?
Ewwww, you stink!

*A tomato and cabbage were walking together down a busy street. They both stepped off the curb and were immediately hit by a speeding car. The tomato was not hurt but called 000 emergency because the cabbage was badly injured. The injured cabbage was taken by ambulance to the hospital and rushed into surgery. After 10 hours of surgery the doctor finally appeared. He said, 'I have good news, and I have bad news. The good news is that your friend the cabbage is going to pull through but the bad news is that he's going to be a vegetable for the rest of his life.'*

**103**

# BURP-
# A-CISE

# THE TOUR DE BURP

The Tour de Burp is a gruelling ride from the mouth to the gut and back again. It is arguably the greatest and most physical gut race in digestive history. This digestive course will encounter features such as:

**Gastroparesis** – Where saliva, spit, drool and dribble rule.

**The Thrilling Throat Bend** – A very sharp downhill hairpin turn with a speed sign of 25 km/hr.

**The Gut Descent** – A narrow, tight, sticky treacherous downhill run, where speeds can exceed 140 km/hr.

**The Gassy Gut Plains** – Warm and moist with blustery liquid gas blasts and eruptions that can happen at any moment.

## The Organ Tour – From previous Tour de

Burps and took in the gall bladder time trial, the pancreatic criterion and the liquid liver flat stage. Fortunately these are no longer in this year's Tour de Burp.

## The Oesophageal Alps – The hardest

uphill climbs are in this section of the Tour. It's a slippery and slimy uphill battle.

# Today's Stage

Today's stage is an out and back from the open mouth caves, through the thrilling throat bend to the gut descent and then into the gassy gut plains for one lap and then the smelleton will make its way up through the Oesophageal Alps and finish in the open-mouthed caves.

## THE RIDERS

Ca-smell Evans (AUS), Belchy Wiggins (UK), Chris Fume (SA), Alburpo Contador (ESP) and Matty Gross (AUS).

The starter burp fires and we are off! Ca-smell Evans and Belchy Wiggins jump to the front to lead out our smelleton. Chris Fume, Alburpo Contador and Matty Gross sit just behind as the riders pedal into the open-mouthed caves. Ca-smell is holding off Belchy as they prepare to start sliding into the throat bend. Ca-smell is pedalling like a demon trying to get some small advantage over Belchy Wiggins before they enter the treacherous murky descent. Riders must cycle furiously to avoid the gnashing teeth, slurping tongue and sticky saliva.

Belchy Wiggins is close behind Ca-smell with both riders being drenched by rivers of wet sticky saliva buffeted by strong gusts of gas. Ca-smell traverses the course with gusto, pedalling past gelatinous membranes and acidic rivers of bile only to become bogged in the intestinal detour. Meanwhile Contador, in his quest for the yellow jersey, inadvertently takes the wrong turn into the gastric bypass and rapidly descends into the catacomb tunnels of intestinal sausage.

As Ca-smell and Belchy break away from the smelleton, they rapidly descend the long narrow Oesophageal Highway, a lonely stretch of wavy sticky pathway, which spits them out into the J-shaped cul-de-sac better known as the 'Chomps de Tummee'.

Caught in their green gassy slipstream are Matty Gross and Chris Fume, who are rapidly gaining on the two breakaways. Their wheels skid and spin as they descend headfirst into a soupy gelatinous puddle. In his attempts to avoid the gastric bypass, Matty Gross loses traction and dives headfirst into a sea of chyme. This gives Fume the chance he has been waiting for and with a gutsy effort he gains on Ca-smell and Belchy.

All three riders now find themselves in the squishy squelchy terrain of the pear-shaped Chomps de Tummee. They must move quickly to avoid the acid and bacterial bath that awaits them.

The stench of methane-smelling decaying food assaults the narrow passages of their nostrils. They put in a mighty effort to climb the long ascent back up through the Oesphageal Highway. This notorious climb will challenge and often break the toughest riders, many of whom have been reduced to burping belching blubbering blobs. There is no easy road as they battle exhaustion and each other to become 'The KING of the Oesophageal Alps', and earn the right to wear the coveted green polka-dot jersey.

Suddenly, by some act of divine indigestion, Ca-smell emerges as the front runner, leading the pack up the last vertical oesophageal climb. It is at this precise moment, just as Ca-smell does a quick check for rivals over his shoulder, that a huge rumbling gaseous blast propels the rest of the smelleton up to his rear wheel. Ca-smell dips his head and pedals with every ounce of power that he has left in his tank.

As the others greedily caress his back wheel, Ca-smell lunges towards the light seeping through the slowly opening lubber lips. He erupts from the gigantic gob in a belching burst to claim the yellow jersey in an ultimate exploding victory.

**VICTORY TO CA-SMELL EVANS –** *Winner of the* **TOUR DE BURP** *'General Disgestification'*

# BUNGEE BURPS

Bungee jumping involves jumping from
a tall structure with an elastic cord tied
around your ankles. The idea is that you
free-fall downwards and just before you hit
the water or ground you are flung up by the
elasticised cord.

Most times all goes well and you recoil skyward
and back down in smaller recoils. At this stage
you compose yourself to make sure no body
fluids or parts have leaked or popped out –
dribble, urine and even eyeballs!

It stands to reason that when free-falling
upside down you would burp – or does it?
Well, many bungee brethren tell us that
when you take the leap of faith off that
bridge your entire body tenses up so tight that
all digestive functions temporarily stop, only burping
when you are upright on land and all of your muscles
and sphincters have relaxed. Good to know that you
don't spray your breakfast in a technicolour belch on the
ground after the initial bungee dive.

# THE BURPIEST SPORTS

## Running

Running is said to produce the most burps and belches, both while doing the activity and afterwards. Scientists cannot pinpoint why exactly but think swallowing air and the lack of blood to the stomach whilst running could be the reason. Blood shunts from the stomach into the legs, heart, lungs and brain when running because that's where it's needed. The thing to note here is not to fight it – better out than in.

## Cycling

Cyclists have to eat and drink during long races. They tend to gulp water as quickly as they can so they won't lag behind. This creates belching bliss because of the large volume of air they gulp. So the Tour de Burp is really a burp-fest.

## Swimming

Swimming is reported to increase burping, especially on an empty stomach. Air is less dense than water so as you gulp a lot of air when swimming your stomach fills up and as they say, it's got to go somewhere – so you burp. The tip here is to hold the belch until after you tumble turn at each end – it will give you acceleration!

## Wrestling

Wrestling is a full-contact sport that involves just about every movement the human body can do. Wrestling combatants force their bodies into twisted and contorted positions which act as a burp and fart pump! The tip here is to make sure you are at the right end!

# Tennis

Tennis players drink copious amounts of water during a match. They can lose between 1.5 and 3 litres of fluid per hour. Drinking so much fluid quickly between sets does rehydrate the player but also causes them to ingest large amounts of air which we know makes you belch. The tip here is to burp loudly to put off your opponent – might as well make it an advantage.

# Race Car Driving

Modern racing drivers have straws fed through their helmets to their mouths from drink bottles below their steering wheel. The stress and G-forces of cornering at 200 kilometres an hour whilst braking and then accelerating has profound extreme effects on breathing. The driver can gulp large amounts of air when cornering as well as between drink slurps, which is the perfect recipe for cooking up big belly burps. The advice here is to stick to the speed limit.

# Yoga

Yoga is an amazing exercise, gentle on the joints and muscles whilst massaging the internal organs. It's great for flexibility and general wellbeing and it's also great at making you fart and burp! The famous position of Downward Dog is the perfect burping platform and launch pad. The tip here is if you go to yoga, always sit at the front where you are not in the fart and burp zone.

# Mountain Climbing

Burping at high altitude is known as High Altitude Flatus Expulsion (HAFE). It commonly happens to mountain climbers and high altitude hikers. The science is simple; as you climb higher there is a decrease in atmospheric pressure, so the pressure created by the intestinal gases becomes much higher than the external pressure, which makes the climber feel the urge to burp and fart. This difference in the external and internal pressure also increases the frequency and volume of burping and farting. If you are compelled to scale the highest coldest mountains in the world, lead the climbing party and then you will avoid being blown off the mountain by the person in front.

# Lawn Bowling

I hear you scoff out loud and say, 'Oh please! Lawn bowls?' Well, lawn bowlers are a very curious and unique breed of game players. They are all ages in the modern game and have been known to drink enormous amounts of carbonated drinks! You know that fizzy drinks make you belch and the more you drink the more you belch. The note here is to follow the saying's advice: 'When in lawn bowl mode, do as the lawn bowlers do.'

# BURPY BUNGEE TRIVIA

- Negative G-force is the pressure of blood rushing towards the head. Positive G-force is the pressure of blood rushing towards your feet and if it becomes too great you faint.
- Bungee jumping is less severe on the human body than many amusement park rides.
- Many people have had their chronic back problems miraculously disappear after doing a bungee jump.
- Bungee jumping has been practised by the 'Danza de Los Vol adores de Papantia' from central Mexico dating back to the Aztecs.
- The 'Land Divers' from the Pentecost Island in Vanuatu are revered as the most famous bungee jumpers. These brave men jump from wooden platforms with vines tied around their ankles as a display of courage and passage into manhood.
- Members of the Oxford Dangerous Sports Club hold the dubious honour of having performed the first modern bungee jumps on 1 April 1979 from the 80-metre-high Clifton Bridge in Bristol, England. The jumpers were arrested and jailed for a few days.

# BUNGEE JOKES

**Q:** Why don't blind people
bungee jump?
**A:** *It scares their guide
dogs senseless.*

**Q:** What did Lady Gaga say
when she burped after her
first ever bungee jump?
**A:** *Mum Mum Mum Mah,
Mum Mum Mum Mah.*

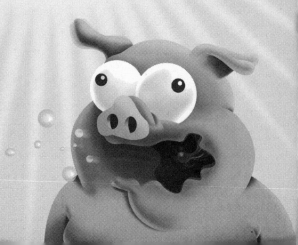

# HALITOSIS

# YOUR BREATH STINKS!

Halitosis is Latin for BAD BREATH! Yes, stinky, smelly, warm, spitty, rotten, rank, belchy, mouth odour. Most body odour is produced by bacteria. Bacteria are all over your body and especially in your gob.

Most people experience 'morning breath', which can be easily fixed by giving your teeth and tongue a good brush and, usually, you are good to go. Unfortunately this doesn't work for a select few people who have what medical types label chronic halitosis. It sounds bad because it is bad – in fact it can be almost impossible to cure.

We are talking breath that is so ripe and rank that it could melt marshmallows at 30 centimetres, breath so stinky it could make a daisy wilt and mouth odour so ridiculously disgusting it could make a small marsupial curl into a ball and roll off down a hill where it would eventually stop, vomit and probably call its mother because it was feeling so sick!

Humans are curious creatures and don't seek out yucky smells, unlike dogs who we know seem to absolutely love the most gross scents and smells. Dogs have a unique greeting ritual – they smell each other's bottoms. I can hear you say ewwwwww gross, but they do and it's probably perfume to them. Luckily, humans don't greet each other with a 'g'day' and then a bottom sniff; it's much quicker to shake hands, which is less smelly, but perhaps not less germ infested … Humans seem to enjoy smells that come from their own bodies, but when smelt on others would make them vomit.

# SMELLY ANOMALIES

**Spit (Saliva)** – Yes, it's true that you actually like the smell of your own spit. After all, it's yours, made in a human saliva factory in your wet warm smelly salty gob.

**Ear Wax** – A curious body secretion that comes in a range of colours! I have heard (nudge nudge – wink wink) that some individuals are quite partial to sliding their pinky finger into their ear and doing a little wax mining. I've been told that it smells like a cross between mildly sweaty socks and waterlogged carpet.

**Belly Button** – The belly button produces two smell anomalies:

1. A colourless, slimy, sticky secretion that sticks to your finger and smells like, for want of a better description, sweaty bottom. The strange thing is that many people have stated that they really enjoy the smell of their belly button. So are they saying that they love the smell of their sweaty bottoms?

2. Belly button fluff, which can be like a mini fluffy ball of stenchy wool or a dark-coloured, hard to remove

crusty little dirt diamond.
Both seem to have a curiously
mesmerising odour that
puts humans into a
chilled out daze.

# Sweaty Armpits

– Sweaty armpits are a multi-billion dollar industry. I hear
you ask how is that possible? Well, millions of people
worldwide use underarm deodorant to combat their
sweaty armpits. Fresh armpit sweat is like your saliva,
mainly salt and fluid which does not smell so bad, but
leave a few hours for the bacteria to do their thing and the
smell goes from salt water to stench county. Your armpits,
like your breath, can also vent the smell of foods you
have eaten such as garlic, onion and curry. Most people
don't like the smell of their own sweat or other people's,
hallelujah!

# The Bottom End – Like the back of a car

where the exhaust comes out, humans have an exhaust as
well – the bottom end. We all know that waste product
comes from here as well as flatus but the bottom end can
also get sweaty and moist, which allows bacteria to have
a feast and produce lots of smells. People are known to
enjoy the smell of their bottom end, whether sweaty or
clean.

I mentioned that humans are a curious species.

# ALARMING BURP AND BREATH SMELLS

## Poo (faeces) Breath – It sounds horrible

and if you have ever had anyone in close proximity breathe or belch poo breath you will know how scarring this can be to your olfactory system. It's almost so disgustingly stinky that your smelling system can shut down like a frozen PC. Fortunately it's not common amongst people. If it was, you couldn't even kiss your lovely nanna on the cheek without having to hold your breath and block your nose.

## Medical Symptoms

**Diabetes** – Strong and sour breath and burps for no reason.

**Kidney failure** – The smell of urine is breathed out.

**Liver failure** – Liver failure is characterised by the smell of fish on the breath even when fish hasn't been consumed.

**Stomach disorders** – Ulcers, GORD and bowel obstruction can make your breath and burps smell of poo.

**Dehydration** – Lack of water can make your mouth dry and high in acid, which makes breath and burps smell like eggs.

**Tonsillitis** – Infected tonsils can increase bacteria and make breath smell like poo.

**Sinus infection** – Post-nasal drip from the back of the nose can increase bacteria and infection and make breath smell like poo.

**Chest infection** – As you cough up the phlegm, which can be full of bacteria, your breath can smell like poo.

# Why do people like their smell?

German biologist Manfred Milinski tells us that liking our smells all starts in our brain. Your brain recognises your own peptides (amino acid) and responds accordingly. When you smell your own burp, fart, sweat or spit, your body recognises these chemical markers and your brain tells us it's 'all good' and you actually enjoy the smell because you've just been told the smell is your own creation made up of your very own DNA.

This is also evident when familiar favourite food is smelled and you feel your stomach rumble or you can even start to salivate. But how is all this related to BURPING? When you burp a big smelly belch and your nose smells it your brain decodes the chemicals and tells you it's you!

So in theory, burping can be used as a weapon! The stench won't make you feel sick but it sure can make others run screaming from the building. FARTING is an even bigger and more potent methane gas-powered weapon – WEAPONS OF GAS DESTRUCTION.

# BURPING TRIVIA

- Did you know that the Egyptians invented the first breath mints? They were made from frankincense, myrrh and cinnamon and boiled with honey. They were then shaped into edible pellets. Do you think Pyramid Mints would take off?

- The US produces about 4 million kilograms of peppermint and spearmint per year.

- Peppermint is one of the oldest and most popular remedies for indigestion.

- Native spearmint is used for toothpaste and dental hygiene products whereas scotch spearmint is more mild and used for chewing gum, sweets and tea.

- The Romans believed that eating mint would make you more intelligent.

- The Romans also believed that eating mint would soothe you and stop you from losing your temper.

- The Hebrews and Christians spread mint on the floors of synagogues and churches as a sign of hospitality.

- The word 'mint' derives from the ancient Greek mythical character Minthe. According to the Greek myth, Minthe was a river nymph. Hades, the God of the underworld, apparently fell head over heels madly in love with river nymph Minthe. The problem was that Hades was married to Persephone and when she found out that her love desired another she cast a spell on Minthe and turned her into a plant. Persephone turned Minthe into a plant because she wanted everyone to walk and trample all over her. Hades could not undo his scorned wife's spell, so Hades gave Minthe a beautiful aroma so when he was near her he could smell her.

# BURPY POEM

## The Ba-a-a-a-urp!

A. JONES

I lay outside on my favourite lounge
My posture semi-prone
Head bent back and eyes are closed
Relaxing on my throne


Summer nights sing their song
Oblivious to me
I am just a single cricket
Resting on a tree


I too can sing a song
That breaks the dead of night
It's a natural melody
That cuts the air with bite


My song is sucked from deep within
Of this I have no choice
The chamber where air is trapped
Way – way down below my voice

The first alert is a little fizz
Followed by a bubble
Then gassy pressure starts to build
I know right then it's trouble

The pressure builds and starts to well
Climbing up my throat
I can't hold it so I let it fly
I belch and bleat like a nanny goat.

# DARE
## TO
# BURP

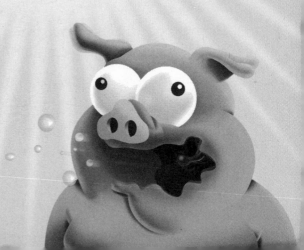

# DARING BURPS
## When burps attack

**WARNING:** This chapter should be used with extreme caution! Only try the following dares when you are in a situation where a little humour is called for ... or when you are feeling really, really naughty!!!!!!

Burps have been used as a weapon for as long as there have been people burping. (Just think about the games you play with your brothers or sisters!) So the time has come for me to share with you my favourite burper behaviour ...

## Naughty Burping Boys ...

- Burp in each other's faces and enjoy the smell!
- Shoot the breeze and fart in public!
- Lick their hand and offer to shake yours!
- Lick their food so they don't have to share it with you!
- Eat the skin they pick off their feet!
- Swap stinky stoinky smelly socks!

# Naughty Burping Girls ...

- Pick that stuff out of their belly buttons and smell it!
- Eat food that's been on the ground longer than the one-minute rule!
- Drink their bath water!
- Belch and giggle and belch and giggle and belch and giggle!
- Pick each other's skin!

# Far Out Fact

Did you know that methane gas is the gas that is produced when you fart? Methane gas is combustible – that means that in the right circumstances methane gas can explode!

# Gas Fact

A man in Holland was undergoing a groin operation and had been put to sleep with an anaesthetic. During the operation the man passed wind (flatulence) and the methane ignited and severely burned his bottom!

# Juicy Jokes

Q: What do you call a boy who doesn't fart in public?
A: *Nothing! They don't exist!*

Q: What do you call a gal who says she doesn't fart?
A: *A big big big fibber!*

# Super Saying

Life is like a fart! It arrives with a bang, sails on the breeze and then just fades away.

# IT'S GROSS & GROTTY YOU BURPING POTTY

If it sounds like a burp and smells like a burp, it must be a burp! Here we go, it's time to get really gross and grotty.

**GG –** Okay, you've been waiting for this one you little grotty monsters! Stand up and load up, and by that I mean prepare to let a raspberry rip! Do a fluff! Do a bottom burp. You know, do a fart! You must do it in front of the whole group! (Gas masks not supplied.)

**GG –** You just did a bottom burp, now you must do a top burp! Stand up tall and burp at least five times. Make them loud and proud!

**GG –** This one is a gasser! For this one you must let someone burp in your face. You are not allowed to block your nose and you must sniff as soon as the burp is born! (Ah ... the sweet smell of mouth!)

**GG** – Smell is one of our most important senses. It alerts us to danger and poisonous odours. It also enables us to smell the wonderful and intoxicating odours of food. Which leads us to our next dare. You know how chicken smells like feet and feet smell like chicken? You got it! Lean over and smell someone's bare foot!!! Really sniff it good so the smell lingers for days!

**GG** – Using your finger of choice, stick it in a nostril (preferably one of your own) and proceed to dig around until you unearth a piece of gold (boogie). When you have the little nose nugget precariously perched on the tip of your finger, hold it out for all to see! Now, in front of everyone assembled, EAT IT!!!

**GG** – Have you ever had an after dinner mint? This one is kind of like an after dinner mint except it tastes like chicken. Take off your shoes and socks, bend over and sniff your feet. Sniff for at least three minutes!

**GG** – Have you got a belly button? If the answer is yes I want you to insert a finger into the deepest recesses of your belly button. Push your finger right in and gently push and probe around until your finger becomes slightly moist! (BINGO!) Now withdraw your finger and sniff it for about one minute!

# TOTAL TRUTHS

Answer these questions completely honestly.

**TT** – Have you ever burped in your little brother's face?

**TT** – Have you ever belched up food into your hands?

**TT** – Have you ever burped and blamed someone else?

**TT** – Have you ever burped and farted at the same time?

**TT** – Have you ever belched in an elevator?

**TT** – Have you ever burped in the car and blamed
someone else?

# SPACE BURPS

# IN SPACE NO ONE CAN HEAR YOU BURP

The big question is … can you burp in space? Yes you can, but they are usually WET! Ewwww. But why are space burps wet I hear you ask? The reason is quite simple – GRAVITY!

We all know that in space astronauts experience zero gravity and this means they float like a feather. This is why space burps are wet. The zero gravity has an effect on the oesophageal sphincter (that valve at the top of your stomach that opens and closes when food goes in and when burps come out).

On Earth, your stomach contents are weighed down due to gravity, whereas in space the contents tend to float at the top of your stomach under your rib cage. Does that sound familiar? Sounds like being on a roller coaster, doesn't it? Do you know that feeling? You're on a roller coaster and drop over the top, your stomach feels like it wants to climb out of your mouth, well that's zero gravity, or to most people 'pre-vomit mode'.

Zero gravity stops the sphincter valve from closing completely, which it does in normal gravity. The effect is when you burp in space the sphincter opens to let the sneaky little belch climb out but doesn't close fully and this is why a little innocent burp in space is really a potential liquid gassy sloppy space soup.

# SOUND IN SPACE

The best part of a burp or belch is the rip-roaring explosiveness of the sound. A burp can be really loud; in fact it can be as loud as a gunshot. On Earth, gravity has an effect on the sound of burping. When you burp on Earth the sound is caused by the vibration of the upper oesophageal sphincter when it seals tightly.

In space, this isn't the case because the upper oesophageal sphincter leaks floating food contents with the gut gas and as a result a wet quiet burp is born. So a space burp is never as loud as an Earth burp.

# DRINKING IN SPACE

Various popular carbonated soft drinks were carried on space missions in 1985. Although these drinks are popular on Earth this is not the case in space.

Carbonated drinks just don't work in space because they increase gut gas which promotes burping and more specifically WET burping or 'space spews' as some people call them. Your tongue swells in space so food and drink needs to have more flavour and drinks can't be carbonated.

Beer companies around the world are trying to perfect a 'space beer' that can be consumed in zero gravity environments. At present, beer is banned on the International Space Station but these companies are preparing for the tourism space travel that will no doubt occur in the near future.

# Did you know?

- Did you know that when they first go into space, astronauts feel quite sick?

- Did you know that astronauts use a special sick bag that has a liner that they can wipe on their face after they have puked into it? It's like an added face wipe so everything goes into the bag. The bag also has a zip-lock on it to stop the vomit from floating around the spacecraft. Imagine five babies in zero gravity; it would be a floating sea of soft sloppy baby food and warm milk! Double ewwwww ...

# MICRO GRAVITY BURP BALLS

When you burp in space you belch out little gassy, soupy, semi-solid balls of food due to the absence of gravity. I know you are thinking, 'Wow, wouldn't a zero gravity room be an awesome attraction at a theme park!' Imagine it, you pay the entrance fee and then sit in a zero gravity fuelling room. A staff member dressed as an astronaut brings you a little plastic tray with three pieces of popcorn, two marshmallows, some chewy lollies, a chunk of chocolate and a small glass of fizzy drink.

You must eat the food quickly and finish it off with the drink. You wait for five minutes as a big clock on the wall counts down and then the doors open and you climb into the zero gravity room.

YUM!

You begin to float around the room belching up your 'astronauts snack'. You then have to 'catch and bag' the contents of your wet-burped zero gravity snack. If you manage to bag all of it you will be awarded a 'zero gravity burp bib'!

## Gassy Funny

**Q:** What do you call a belching astronaut?
**A:** *A gastronaut.*

# BURPY POEM

## Fluffy Gas Pillows

A. JONES

*Fluffy gas pillows that float above me*

*Fluffy so fluffy, as fluffy as can be*

*Burps are gas pillows, fluffy and soft*

*Pixies and elves use them to stay aloft.*

# THE WET BURP

# TWB

The Wet Burp (TWB) is a belching variation on a theme. Well it's really just a burp with soupy sloppy extras. It can be caused by indigestion, gastric reflux, spicy food, eating too much, bending over, lifting heavy things or even laying flat in bed.

Sometimes people are startled when they are gifted with a sour acidic mouthful of gastric juice after a little sneaky burp. But we say never fear the wet burp, it is a gift from your gut.

Wet burps are also known as:

**The 'Derp'** – Dry burp
**The 'Verp'** – Vomit plus burp
**The 'SSS'** – Semi-solid & sloppy
**The 'Werp'** – Wet plus burp
**The 'Lelch'** – Liquid plus belch
**The 'B-Flux'** – Burp plus gastric juice reflux
**The 'Slurp-Dunk'** – Burp plus solid food matter

# FIVE WICKED WET-BURP FOODS

1. **The Milky Slurp** – Milk is a wicked wet burp ingredient. Warm milk is even better. Warm some milk, drink it quickly and prepare to do a milky werp.

2. **The Cornflake Fling** – Cornflakes have a habit of sticking to everything in odd shapes, sizes and textures. They are the perfect partner in crime to milk for creating a totally amazing SSS!

3. **The Sloup** – Soup is a wet burp staple. It must be a completely liquid broth with no chunky veggie inclusions. It can be any type of soup that you like. Sloup is semi-sloppy, not too viscous (thick), liquid belch fuel for making a tasty lelch.

4. **The Sloup Plus –** This the same as the sloup but with the added inclusion of veggies – little chunks of pumpkin, potato, peas and of course that amazing vegetable phenomenon that is the carrot! This is your absolute first choice for creating a slurp-dunk. Boo ya!

5. **The Bean Bloop –** Baked beans on toast is almost the perfect food as we know they can make the body produce gas AND wind. They will definitely give you a quick fix of gut gas and sometimes those little semi-hard, kidney-shaped fibre diamonds will add extra fibre to your burps! Definitely a slurp-dunk.

# THE RUCTUS RETREAT

Here are some ways to reduce the ructus (burping and belching).

**RR 1 –** Avoid carbonated drinks. Fizzy drinks are PURE BELCHING FUEL.

**RR2 –** Eat and drink slowly, as gulping air will bloat you and make you a belching machine (not that there is anything wrong with that).

**RR3 –** There is a reason why you shouldn't talk with your mouth full! It causes you to gulp excess air, which makes you belch.

**RR4 –** Avoid acidic food such as oranges, grapefruit and vinegar.

**RR5** – Limit spicy food such as pepper and chilli.

**RR6** – Limit your chewing gum intake as it's a sure-fire way to gulp lots of air because you swallow more often than normal.

**RR7** – Sip from a glass and don't use a straw. Using a straw is like a mixer tap of air and fluid.

**RR8** – Try to avoid huge yawns. Yawning will make you swallow huge amounts of air.

**RR9** – The most contentious ructus-reducing advice is to reduce your intake of mousses (the dessert, not the animal), soufflés and whipped cream. NOT fair!

The famous British astronomer and mathematician Sir Isaac Newton coined the phrase, 'What goes up must come down' after an apple fell from a tree. We Burptopians say, 'What goes in, must come out', which should not be confused with the Aussie version which is, 'Better out than in'.

# THE WET BURP CHALLENGE

It's time to separate the burpers from the amateurs with these wet burp challenges.

- Try to make up five of your own your wicked wet burp concoctions. They can be designed or concocted from anything you eat or drink.

- Make a list of your wet burps (see the categories on page 152) as well as noting which burp came after the food you ate – you will be amazed by what you will discover.

- Record every time you see carrot or anything carrot-like in a wet burp.

BLURRPSH........

- Record the ratio of wet burps to dry burps.

# WET BURPY TRIVIA

- Did you know that babies are the champions of the WET burp? Most of the food they eat is sloppy and soupy, just perfect for wet burping. They also suck in a lot of air with the milk they drink, as well as having underdeveloped oesophageal muscles. Babies need to be burped and gently patted on the back. But don't pat too hard, as that can mean more wet burping!

- Did you know that the book *Charlie and the Chocolate Factory* features a whole section dedicated to burping? Go and check it out immediately. I'll wait.

# THE
# WORLDWIDE
# BURP

# BURPY POEM

## Burptionality

A. JONES

It's quite absurd how people burp

the noises that they make

Some are known to slop and slurp

in public for goodness sake!

We all know humans will let one go

it is a natural act

some will try and put on a show.

They have a special knack

Attention seekers at the front

Shy guys go behind

Belch and burpers sigh and grunt

Happy with their kind.

# BURPING ETIQUETTE AROUND THE WORLD

Did you know burping is seen by some cultures as a natural process that is good for your physical, spiritual and mental well-being? It is accepted and almost customary to belch loudly after a nice meal in some Asian countries such as India, China and Vietnam. It is considered a sign of gastronomic satisfaction, almost like applauding the chef or cook with your burp.

Germans consider a burp after a meal of sauerkraut and sausage a compliment to the chef as well. In fact, it is considered rude if guests do not belch their appreciation, which is seen as a long-held tradition.

In the Arab world, burping is not socially shared or enjoyed. A story passed on says that a man burped in the presence of the prophet Salla Allahu Aleihi Wa Sallam. The prophet looked directly into the man's eyes and said, 'Hold your burping away from us, those who are most satiated in this life will be the most hungry ones in the hereafter.'

# India

In India, the louder the burp the better. Indians enjoy and encourage letting a huge pappadum pop out after a delicious meal. It shows that you CARE!

# Japan

The Japanese saying goes, 'Slurp but not burp' so it's ok to vigorously slurp and suck your miso or ramen soup with your bowl perched under your chin, but burping is considered rude.

# China

The Chinese have been allowed to 'slurp 'n' burp' for thousands of years. This relaxed custom is seen as a way to show appreciation of a meal.

# France

Who would believe that a progressive country like France would be shy about burping at the table? Well, they are, I'm afraid. Don't burp at the table or NO crème brûlée for you!

# Italy

The Italians don't like burps to be heard, which is a contradiction because the Italians are not exactly a quiet race. Think opera singer Pavarotti, Ferrari racing cars or that Italian guy screaming out at the fruit market.

# United Kingdom

The British regard burping as a rude and crude gesture – unless you are at a football match.

# Canada

It's a custom to burp after a meal in Canada and it's also a sport in Canada, which is where the World Burping Championship has been held. Those crafty Canadians have given the world the winter sports of hurling and ice hockey as well as burping!

# Australia

Aussies are known for their relaxed attitude and this is proven by the BBQ Burp, which is an indication that you have enjoyed the sausage on bread at the sausage sizzle. They do still expect a polite, 'Excuse me' if you let out a burp at the dinner table.

# BURPS OF THE WORLD
## Give belch a chance

It's a distinct advantage to know how to say 'burp' in other languages. It can save you much embarrassment and also explain the difference between gas and a grunt!

**Arabic**   *Dasheshur* (pronounced **Da shyes shur**)

**Chinese**   *Dage* (pronounced **Da-gurr**)

**Danish**   *Bovs* (pronounced **Bose**)

**Dutch**   *Boeren* (pronounced **Boo er**)

**French**   *Roter* (pronounced **Row**)

**German**       *Rulpser* (pronounced **Rulp sir**)

**Italian**      *Rutto* (pronounced **Roo toe**)

**Japanese**     *Geppo* (pronounced **Ge-pooh**)

**Latin**        *Ructo* (pronounced **Ruc toe**)

**Malay**        *Sendawa* (pronounced **Sen dow wa**)

**Polish**       *Bekniecie* (pronounced **Bec knee oh cha**)

**Russian**      *Akriska* (pronounced **Are chris car**)

**Spanish**      *Eructo* (pronounced **EH ructo**)

**Swedish**      *Erack* (pronounced **E rack**)

**Turkish**      *Gegirme* (pronounced **Gear meh**)

**Vietnamese**   *Tieng* (pronounced **Tea ung up**)

# BURPTOPIA
# A place where a burp is a kiss

Located to the north of Fartopia and to the south of Upper Nostril Snozola lies the picturesque country of Burptopia! It's a land where they speak in 'burp tongue,' a language officially known as Burpish. It is a language driven by gassy guttural grunts and moans, which to the Burptopians sounds like a perfect melody.

Burptopia is ruled over by Baron Belcher the 5th, whose family is worshipped for their unique burping abilities. They can even burp and belch underwater.

Burptopia has some very unique and interesting customs.

- Burptopians greet each other with a smile, handshake and a full burp to the FACE.
- Burptopians don't cheer, they BELCH in harmony with each other as seen at the Burptopian Games.
- Burptopians show appreciation to others for the loudness and duration of burps (the louder the burp the more appreciated they are).
- The Burptopian motto is 'BELCH and LET BELCH'.
- Burptopians consider it RUDE to eat with your mouth closed.
- Burptopians believe the greatest gift you can give is to regurgitate a WET burp into the palm of your hand and offer it to another.

# Famous Burptopians

**Justin Belcher** – Singer who had a hit with the song 'Baby Baby Bay Burp'.

**One Indigestion** – A very popular boy band discovered on a Burptopian talent show.

# Famous Burptopian Sports

**Hurling** – The Burptopian version is a vomiting contest.

# National Animal

Burptopians idolise their triple-humped camel, it is their national animal revered for its incredibly smelly burps!

BRRRUP!

# BURP ARTISTS

# BURP ART

Leonardo de Belchy, Pablo Pigasso, Remburp, Edgar De-gas, Vincent van Gas and Pro Fart are all famous artists. You too can be a famous artist. Just keep reading for some tips on creating your own 'Work of Burps'.

## Top Ten Burp Masterpieces

Make sure you label your drawings so you get the credit.

**BM1** – Design a type of transport that is powered by burp gas.

**BM2** – Design a burp that might be used to help someone get out of a tricky situation.

**BM3** – Draw an electric-powered burp.

**BM4** – Design a burp machine that might help people in their daily lives.

**BM5** – Draw a BURP-TOO, a burp tattoo design.

**BM6** – Draw some of your own burps. (Use your imagination to think up what they look like.)

**BM7** – Design a futuristic burp machine that might help power a planet.

**BM8** – Design a new invention that uses burp power in some way.

**BM9** – Draw a comic strip featuring your invisible burp friend.

**BM10** – Draw a burp masterpiece. This can be anything you want it to be (as long as it's gassy).

NOTE – Your burp masterpieces can incorporate anything that is related to burping. They can include people, places, funny situations or events. You can draw and create new inventions that are powered by air, burp, bubbles, wet burps, belching babies or any type of burp-related sound or subject. You're only limited by your own gassiness.

# Advanced Burp Masterpiece Challenges

Time to take it to the next artistic level!

**ABM 1** – Design a Happy Burp-day card.

**ABM 2** – Design a poster advertising the benefits of burps. Try to include a catchy slogan, for example 'Burps Make You Better'.

**ABM 3** – Design a travel brochure for the fictional country Burptopia (see pages 167–169).

**ABM 4** – Design a trophy for the Tour de Burp (see pages 106–111).

**ABM 5** – Design a burping baby bib for your little sister or brother.

**ABM 6** – Create your own burping stickperson calendar.

**ABM 7** – Design and label your very own 'Burp Collection Device' such as a puke pack, burp basket, belch bag or hiccup handbag.

# Did you know?

- Did you know that the famous artist Leonardo de Belchy who created the Mona Lisa painted it just after she had eaten a huge plate of Italian baked beans? The name Mona is based on the word 'moaner'. It was derived from the belching sound she made after consuming the huge plate of gas-producing beans.

(The source for this fact is now currently being investigated by art authorities from around the world and was last seen boarding a flight to Burptopia.)

# BURP ACTIVITIES

Here are some fun activities to keep you busy on a rainy (or windy) day. They are guaranteed to beat the burping blues with hours of gassy, gut-blasting belching fun.

**BA 1 –** Try to name every single one of your burps, for example the Super Stinky, the Belching Bomb, The Goo Goo Gas No 1. etc.

**BA 2 –** Count how many burps you do in one hour.

**BA 3 –** Write down what time you do the loudest and quietest burps.

**BA 4 –** Time how long your burps last.

**BA 5 –** Burp in a few different rooms in your house and try to work out which room allows you to do the loudest burp. Think about why this might be.

**BA 6 –** Burp standing up and then lying down. Take note of which burp is louder and which lasts longer.

**BA 7 –** Have a burping competition with your friends – give prizes for the longest, the loudest, the smelliest etc.

**BA 8 –** Burp out as many letters of the alphabet as you can.

# BURPY POEM

## Burps Are ...

A. JONES

Burps are ...
  Gassy
    Gushy
      and
        Sometimes Mushy

Burps are ...
  Loud
    Low
      and
        from Somewhere Below

Burps can ...
  Blow
    Blast
      and
        Erupt Super Fast

Burps are ...
  Wet
    Soppy
      and
        Oh so sloppy

Burps are ...
  Stinky
    Smelly
      and
        From Your Belly

Burps are ...
  Bodacious
    Fantastic
      and
        Totally Bombastic!

# BELCHOGA – BURPING YOGA

# THE CREATION OF GASSY MASTERPIECES

There is an ancient Belchoga chart that was found in Burptopia thousands of years ago. It is a copy of the original Burptopian Belchoga guide to the most effective and relaxing ways to position the human body for maximum burping and belching.

The Burtopians believed that burping and belching was a gift from the heavens that was sacred and should be shared, practised and perfected by all who lived in Burptopia. Even though Belchoga has been practised for thousands of years in Burptopia it has only recently found its way to the modern day.

## Ancient Egyptians

The ancient Egyptians adapted Belchoga and

called it Pharaoh Belching. It was modelled and practised by the Pharaohs and their people and involved very angular body shapes that the Egyptians thought promoted burping. If you look at a picture of an Egyptian sphinx you can see the direct relationship between the sphinx's pose and Pharaoh Belching position No 1.

# Ancient Greeks

The ancient Greeks also enjoyed a version of Belchoga. 'Acroppolloptiuptius' was a very popular form of Belchoga reputed to have been designed by the Greek gods and flown to Earth by the Greek Goddess Bur-pees, the Goddess of Gas! Legend tells us that she flew under the cover of night to every household and delivered the Acroppolloptiuptius movements into the dreams of every sleeping mother in Greece. The story also tells how on the same day at exactly the same time all mothers in Greece awoke and the first thing they did was wake up their children and try these poses.

# Ancient Romans

The ancient Romans also enjoyed their version of Belchoga called Colosqueeseum Indigestium. It was practised and accepted as the second most popular pastime to watching the Gladiators. Colosqueeseum Indigestium was a less vigorous form of Belchoga with more emphasis on the look of the pose as opposed to the effectiveness of it. The Romans adapted it after seeing it done by the Germanic army years earlier in battle. The Romans developed a mix of Egyptian Pharaoh belching and Germanic mass burping and mixed it with tomatoes and pasta to form their unique set of poses.

# Bondi Body Boogie

The newest variation of Belchoga was created by partygoers at Bondi Beach on 1 January 1961. Many partygoers who had spent New Year's Eve revelling at Bondi Beach had woken to the most amazing sunrise and were so taken with the beauty and serenity of this spectacle that they stood up and started to stretch towards the heavens. This mass movement was named Bondi Body Boogie Belch because it incorporated dance moves with yoga positions that made you burp. Some people have speculated that it was specifically designed to

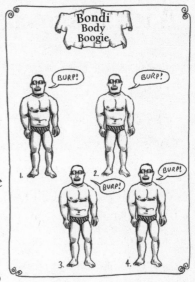

help rid the body of excess gas from the previous night while others say it was born from a moment of beauty on a beach full of synchronised souls.

**Every version of Belchoga can be used by people of any age, sex or nationality who feel they have an excess of gas built up in their stomach with a need, a need to BURP!**

# BURP
# -SPEAK

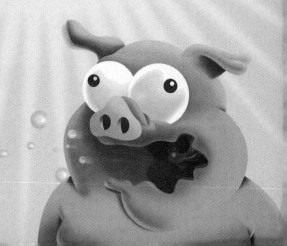

# THE SPOKEN BURP

Think about that kid at school who can burp the alphabet, that one gifted individual that every school in every city in every state in every country has, who has mastered the art of burp speak. It is quite a unique ability that is envied by many a primary school student. Burp-speak is a crowd-pleasing, person-teasing, teacher-menacing classroom gift and when performed at the right time can send a classroom full of kids into fits of uncontrollable laughter and drive teachers totally crazy.

Hel-BURP! lo! How -URP! ARRURRP YOUURRPP!!!

Like most talents, burp-speak has to be nurtured and practised to fully develop its powerful potential. It must only be used in moderation – if used too much, its amazing comical effect will wear off. As they say in showbiz, 'It will get old and stale like bread, which of course will then become a green and mouldy fungi, and this mouldy green fungi on the bread then becomes penicillin which can be taken in pill form to treat many bacterial infections in the human body, and of course if penicillin is taken for too long it can make you burp!' It always comes back to the burp!

# HOW DO YOU BURP-SPEAK?

Here are some tips to get you started burp-speaking.

1. **The Alphabet** – A classic crowd pleaser, you can Burp from A–Z and from Z–A!

A B C D E F G H I J K L M N O P Q R S T U V W X Y Z
Z Y X W V U T S R Q P O N M L K J I H G F E D C B A

2. **Knock Knock Jokes** – There are many to choose from and most work well when burp spoken.

*Knock Knock*
*Who's there?*
*Tank.*
*Tank who?*
*You're welcome.*

*Knock Knock*
*Who's there?*
*Abbey.*
*Abbey who?*
*Abbey Birthday.*

*Knock Knock*
*Who's there?*
*Omer.*
*Omer who?*
*Omer goodness wrong door.*

**3. Pig Jokes –** Pig jokes sound funnier when burp-spoken as it adds to the gruntiness and impact of the gag.

**Q:** Where do pigs go for holidays?
**A:** *Hamster-dam.*

**Q:** What is a pig's favourite sport?
**A:** *Ham ball.*

**Q:** What do pigs call their grandfathers?
**A:** *Ham pa.*

4. **Poems** – Poetry is one of the best things to burp-speak because it has great rhythm and rhyme.

> The sky is blue
> The sun is yellow
> This joke was made
> By a brain of jello.
> > A. Jones

> A woolly jumpered kangaroo
> And two white rabbits skating through.
> Collide out back with such a thump
> Sounds like a hop, squeak and a jump.
> > A. Jones

5. **Limericks** – Limericks are great to burp-speak because they cover so many topics but always have the same rhyme scheme. The rhyme is AABBA, so the first two lines must rhyme, then the next two lines must rhyme, then the final line must rhyme with the first line.

> There was a small boy nicknamed 'De Slurp'
> They say he was born in Antwerp
> He loved to belch loud
> He belched for the crowd
> This belching twerp who could burp.

**6. Movie Quotes** – Movies provide the burp-speaker with an endless library of amazing lines and quotes. Start with your favourite line from your favourite film.

**7. Spoken Burp Quickies** – Quickly state your full name, age and address.

**8. Traditional or Modern Rhymes** – Belch these out.

- Peter picked a piece of pickled peppercorn.
- She sells seashells by the seashore.

# BURP-SINGING

Burp singing is just like burp speaking with the only difference being that you burp-sing instead of burp-speak the words. Singing with burp power is a little more difficult than burp speaking. You need to have much more gas loaded and ready to support a burp song.

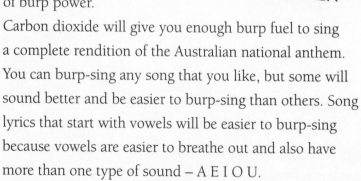

You can load up with a fizzy drink which will give you plenty of burp power.

Carbon dioxide will give you enough burp fuel to sing a complete rendition of the Australian national anthem. You can burp-sing any song that you like, but some will sound better and be easier to burp-sing than others. Song lyrics that start with vowels will be easier to burp-sing because vowels are easier to breathe out and also have more than one type of sound – A E I O U.

# BURPY TRIVIA

- Did you know that one of the longest and most memorable movie burps is delivered by a character named 'Booger' in the 1984 film *Revenge of the Nerds*? It only lasts about 7 seconds but is regarded as one of the most beast-like belches ever filmed.

- Did you know that the Inuit people of Canada burp loudly after a meal as a sign of thanks and also to show that the food was really enjoyable?

- Excessive burping not related to food or drink consumption can be a symptom of a heart attack. People sometimes present at an emergency room with burping as the only symptom.

- Did you know that there are many restaurants with the word 'burp' in the name? Here are some famous ones:
Burp Town – Mumbai, India
Burps & Giggles Cafe and Restaurant – Ipoh, Malaysia
Cafe Burps – Pune, India
Burp Eat Drink – Queensland, Australia
Burp – Adelaide, Australia
Burp Castle – New York, USA

# JOBS THAT MAKE YOU GO BURP

# BEST BURPING PROFESSIONS

This information was provided by the International Burp and Belch Council for the Equal Retention and Expulsion of Gas in the Workplace. Statistics criteria included FOB (Frequency of Burp), VOB (Volume of Burp), POB (Pungency of Burp), BPD (Burps per Day), BPH (Burps per Hour) and BPM (Burps per Minute). All statistics were collected in a humane manner.

## Sports Team Coach

Coaches spend training sessions, planning sessions and game days screaming and shouting at players, coaching staff, medical staff, referees, opposing fans, supporting fans, animals that fly or walk onto the sports field, the weather, imaginary people and even at themselves! All of that screaming, yelling and shouting takes enormous amounts of inhaled and gulped air and this is where the coach becomes the Belching Beast that instils fear in all who stand near him or her. Coaches ranting have been known to start choruses of crying babies up to one kilometre away.

Gulping large amounts of air when a person is really aggressive and excited will fill them up with hot air. Sometimes you get a TV camera shot of a coach in a box behind glass exploding with rage and luckily you can't hear them, but you can bet your life that they end up being a red-faced, crimson-tempered belching beastie!

### BURPING BY PROFESSION TIP (BBPT)

If you are playing in a team and the opposing side scores, make sure you are as far away from the coach as possible, his or her screaming and burping could cause hearing damage.

At halftime when the team has a meeting inside or on the ground, do not stand directly in front of the coach when he or she is speaking. If the coach comes in close to have a face-to-face chat with you, look down immediately, as the coach's stress burps could slap you smack bang in the middle of the face and possibly turn your face to stone.

# Auctioneer

The loudest most rapid-fire babbling burping beast to ever splutter up to 400 words a minute is the auctioneer. Auctioneers sell just about anything, from cars to castles, cows to couches, artwork to ancient antiquities as well as jewellery, clothes, shoes, toys and even dolls.

The auctioneer is regarded as one of the quickest speakers on the planet. They need to verbally repeat the dollar amounts of the goods they are auctioning as the price increases. They speak quickly in the same monotone way so people listening and bidding for items know exactly what the last bid was. They also repeat numbers and key words throughout the auction and must deliver them quickly to keep people motivated and interested in bidding. People have described the auctioneer in full verbal flight as sounding like an hypnotic didgeridoo. Auctioneers inhale huge amounts of air in microseconds between blasts of words, the sheer quantity of which makes them belch like wild African wilderbeasts.

---

### BURPING BY PROFESSION TIP (BBPT)

Don't under any circumstances ask an auctioneer for directions if you are lost. Your ears will be assaulted with the most rapid-fire verbal blast ever known, which will end with a burp in your face. You will be left in a cloud of gut gas and more confused than before you asked. Instead, get a GPS unit.

If you happen to be at a party or function do not ask an auctioneer what they have been doing lately. This is asking for aural destruction! The auctioneer will burp out hundreds of words a minute that will have you scratching your head. Not only will you not understand what he or she has said but you might even end up in a state of slight hypnosis with didgeridoo ringing in your ears. Don't risk it.

---

# Chef

A chef is in the unique position of providing sustenance, joy and happiness to all people. Think about it, which other job can provide arguably the two greatest joys in life – cooking and eating. These joys can be shared in any setting, by any age group, anywhere in the world. Chefs also get to work with great ingredients and tools that change the raw produce into edible culinary delights.

Burping can be a problem for a chef as all chefs have to taste the food at each stage of cooking, usually tasting small mouthfuls throughout the complete cooking process. This constant tasting and swallowing also sucks in excess air, which makes the chef a burper of note. Some chefs call these occupational burps Culinary Tweets, Gastric Flourishes or Belch a Baisse.

### BURPING BY PROFESSION TIP (BBPT)

Never stand directly in front of a chef just after they have finished preparing a gourmet meal triumph as you will be in the Culinary Tweet Zone and blasted with Gastric Flourishes before being finished off with Belch a Baisse burps. In other words, you will get to feel the warmth and smell of every ingredient that went into the meal!

When you are cooking up a storm and of course tasting all the way, be aware that you are loading up on Gastric Flourishes. You can discreetly release them by turning your head left and right whilst engaged in conversation at the dinner table or you can ease them out with stealth-like precision and let your gut gas do all the talking.

# The Politician

Nothing on Earth, with the exception of a huge hot-air balloon, contains as much hot air as that dog-patting, baby-holding, grandma-kissing, publicity-grabbing creature known as the politician. Their gift is the ability to take in information, facts and figures, turn it into hot air and expel it as wind which has been changed into totally inaccurate, twisted and unreliable belch.

Politicians are hot-air-making machines, their power source is seemingly endless – so much so that they could single-handedly power a small nation! Politicians also love to make speeches and to listen to the sound of their own voices and burps.

**BURPING BY PROFESSION TIP (BBPT)**

Never stand too close to a politician as he or she will suck all the available air and you will feel giddy and dizzy.

If you ever go to a political party meeting always take an oxygen mask with you because with that many politicians in one room breathable air will become scarce.

# The Taste Tester (Super Taster)

The taste tester is someone who is employed specifically to assess the flavour of foods and drinks. Most taste testers have a highly developed sense of taste and go by the title of super tasters. Taste tasters are employed to taste absolutely everything that humans eat, some are even specialised in areas such as cheese, chocolate, water, wine and beer.

The super taster who tastes carbonated drinks exclusively is the belching master! Every time a sample of carbonated drink is swilled, swallowed or spat out, burp fuel is instantly made. The carbonated drink super taster is a weapon of gas destruction! Stand in close at your own peril. If you love to burp and belch and never knew that you could do it for a career then this could be the profession for you.

## BURPING BY PROFESSION TIP (BBPT)

If you are at an exclusive carbonated drink tasting, stand to the left side of a super taster as they always turn their heads to the right to release a post-taste belch. Remember, this person is a weapon of gas destruction and people could get hurt!

If you are at a birthday party always make sure that you are standing higher than all of your friends after they start slurping down the fizzy drinks. Height is your friend and will absolutely stop you from being gas gobsmacked from a carbonated slurping buddy.

# NOTABLE BURPING PROFESSIONS

These professions are definitely worth a mention.

## Tennis Player

Tennis players guzzle so much water and bounce around on court that they make much more gas than you would believe. How many times have you seen a tennis star interviewed after the game and they can only speak between burps? Tennis players are masters of the wet and squishy burp, the gut volley!

# School Principal

As we all know, school principals love the sound of
their own voices and will speak to the school at any
opportunity. They share some similarities with politicians
as they take in large amounts of air, warm it and then
belch it out in the form of instructions, announcements
and of course words of wisdom related to school
procedure. No one has done any scientific tests on how
much hot air and burps principals produce but, like
politicians, they never seem to run dry.

# Sports Announcer

Whether on TV, radio or online, sports announcers get so
involved and excited in the call that they swallow huge
amounts of air, which gurgles around in their gut and
makes a second-half belching comeback.

# BURPING
# BRETHREN

# BURPING PERSONALITY TYPES
## Which burper are you?

The world is packed to the gassy gills with many types of burping machines. Read and see if you are one of the species below.

**The Beast** – The beast will belch anywhere, anytime in front of anyone, even the queen!

**The Proud Father** – This burper blows one out like a trumpet and then smiles at everyone, like he has created something special, amazing and beautiful.

**The Public Menace** – The public menace likes to blast out a blindingly loud belch at any opportunity, and always at the most inappropriate moment. He or she uses burps as a tool to make people laugh, but we all know who the real tool is.

**The Worrier** – The worrier burper is nervous like a little mouse, skittish like a little bird and trembles like a chihuahua. The worrier lets out squeaky little burps anytime he or she feels nervous about anything.

**The Idiot** – Idiots like to burp, then giggle, then burp again, then giggle again, then burp again and giggle some more. Do you need to know more?

**The Belcheologist** – Like an archeologist and a farteologist, this person has the ability to dig deep and extract that burp from the farthest, deepest and darkest reaches of the intestinal tract and release it into the unsuspecting world.

**The Romantic** – A true romantic believes in love, but a romantic burper just believes in burps. They get all misty eyed after letting one go.

**The Baby** – This person has no control over when and where a burp is released and it can be wet, dry and smelly. They're cute though, so we forgive them.

**The Ring-in** – As soon as someone else burps, the ring-in joins in – never the first but always the second.

**The Nanna** – Old age is hard going and nobody knows that better than Nanna. Every time she moves forwards, backwards, right or left, she burps. This can be caused by gas build-up when sitting still, stomach problems or just Nanna not caring.

**The Mutant** – Strange individual, this one, the mutant will burp and then tilt its head back with eyes open wide almost bulging and stare at you with a contorted and twisted face as though waiting for you to say something.

# BURP SPECIES

Burps come in different lengths, sounds and volume. Check out the burp species below and see which categories yours fall into.

**The Barp** – Sounds like a short sharp BARP! Exactly like its name.

**The Frog** – Sounds like a single frog croak, short duration and almost sounds sharp.

**The Toad** – Sounds fuller, lower and more resonant than the frog, also sounds a little meaner.

**The Big Bang** – Sounds like a gut explosion without the vomit, usually very warm as it's born.

**The Gob Smack** – Sounds like a scllllllllap in the face, lots of air involved.

**The Choke Croak** – Sounds longer than most burps and almost like it's slightly choked.

**The Blurp** – Sounds like the barp but with a 'ler' sound after the 'B'. It has a longer duration than the barp.

**The Wet Belch** – Sounds like a full-bellied, full-bodied wet blarp!

**The Cave Brrrrrr** – Sounds almost like a long lion roar from deep within a cave.

**The Ructus Rampage** – Sounds like wet and dry rapid-fire burps, lots of burps and many different sounds.

**The Bark Burp** – Sounds like a moderate dog bark without the 'B' sound, almost like 'Arkkk' (no, not Noah's).

**The Wurp** – Sounds exactly like its name, it starts with a 'Wwwwww'. Babies do it a lot, it's not loud and it's usually wet.

**The Dead Gut** – Sounds like any burp on the list but the difference is that it absolutely stinks! The smell is so bad people nearby ask if something died here.

# THE BLAME GAME
# (Who me? No way!)

Now that you know what type of burper you are and the types of burps you do, you can play the blame game.

**The Mouth Guard** – If you are in a confined space with a group of people (elevator, bus, train etc.) and need to burp out a big bang belch, raise your hand to your mouth, cover your mouth but don't seal it, open your hand so it looks covered but it's actually not then blow out a big one and immediately look to the person next to you before everyone looks around. Works every time. As you leave the group raise your right arm above your head and say, 'So long suckers.'

## The 'Did You Hear That?' – This is great if you

are with one or two people, the idea is to distract them by saying, 'Did you hear that?' and then looking somewhere so they follow your gaze. It takes nerves of steel to pull the 'Did you hear that?' off. Remember, do not burp directly at any person, burp in another direction and then turn and motion in the opposite direction and say it.

## Ignorance Is Bliss – The trick here is to act totally

and completely oblivious to the belch. Make sure you belch straight ahead without opening your mouth too wide and then look away like you are daydreaming. Someone might say, 'What was that?' You should turn to them and mumble, 'What?' Works a treat and the whole affair is left in the burp-muda triangle.

## Blame Nanna – If you are at a family gathering and

dislodge and blow out a huge burple, blame it on Nanna. Say, 'Whoaaaaaa Nanna, that was a big burp!' and lean towards her. Nanna won't react and to be honest probably cannot hear that well so your words will fall on deaf ears, literally. If her hearing is good she will probably agree with you and say, 'Yes dear I get gas.' It's a win-win and no one gets hurt.

## 'You Wouldn't Believe What Happened to Me' – If you let out an unscheduled gut-busting belch you can divert attention by blurting out some bizarre random comment. Start it with, 'You wouldn't believe what happened to me on the way here today …' Proceed to tell a completely crazy story. Interrupt your own story to say you have to go to the bathroom and make a getaway. You will leave them hanging to hear what happened and your burp has yet again gone into the burp-muda triangle.

## Blame the Dog – A classic, this one always works like a charm. Everyone expects dogs to release loud sounds and stinky stenchy odours, so the dog is the perfect blame victim. Dogs do burp but cats don't, so this is only good for dogs. As soon as you belch out a burp, look at the pooch and say, 'Naughty dog, that was the biggest, meanest burp that I have ever heard you do, what have you been eating, hmmm?'

**Blame Yourself** – As soon as you burp, blame
yourself and your stomach. You must talk about your
stomach like it doesn't belong to you, as though it's a
third person or organ of sorts. Speak about how gassy
you are and how much gas you've had all day. Start to go
into explicit detail about your belches, explain to those
around you their frequency, volume and even how much
they smell! They will soon move away and you will be left
alone with the smelly remnants of your burp, content in
the knowledge that you blamed your stomach and fooled
them all.

# BURPY POEM

## We Are Gathered Here Today

A. JONES

We are gathered here today, gathered here today,

To talk about the burp, let's talk about the burp

We are gathered here today, yes gathered here today

To talk about the burp, let's talk about the burp

We are gathered here today, gathered here today

To talk about the burp, let's talk about the burp.

# BURPING
# THE
# ZODIAC

# WHAT IS A RUMINANT?

Ruminants are mammals that have four-chambered stomachs and two-toed feet. I know at this very moment you are wondering if your little brother is a ruminant. Well, he may eat like he has a four-chambered stomach and have feet that cannot be classified because they're never identified without sweaty socks on, but sadly he is not a ruminant, he is just a smelly, icky, sticky creature that eats more than his body weight.

Ruminants eat quickly and store the food in their first stomach, which is called the rumen. The food softens and is called cud. The cud is later regurgitated back into their mouth and chewed again. Cud is then swallowed and sent to the other chambers of the stomach – the reticulum, omasum and abomasum where the food is digested with other micro-organisms.

There are about 150 domestic and wild ruminant species but there are only 12 species in the Ruminant Zodiac. Each species in the Ruminant Zodiac has specific characteristics that can also be shared by humans. Just as zodiac star signs tell us specific characteristics about people born on certain days in certain months, the Ruminant Zodiac can do the same. So check out which ruminant star sign you are.

## The Cow 21 March–21 April

People born under the ruminant king of the cowpat are blessed with super belching ability. They also have the capacity to make upwards of 300 litres of methane gas per day, which is a lot of burping. They have a natural ability to belch, burp and fart and like to socialise in large groups, move in large groups and of course moo in large groups.

**BURP VALUE – 10 Bps**

# The Sheep 21 April–21 May

Those born under the sign of the sheep are quiet, shy and can be quite hairy! They are usually completely covered in wool from head to toe, which can be a problem in summer. They need to have their incredible coat of hair sheared or shaved completely once a year to combat overheating. They often wear large gold necklaces that sit on their natural thickets of woolly lush undergrowth. Traditionally not the most intelligent sign, they always follow the leader in the flock but never really know who that is. They can be quite nervous and will run with no idea of where or why they are running. They burp very quietly but can output about 100 litres of gut gas a day.

**BURP VALUE – 9 Bps**

## The Goat 21 May–21 June

The sign of the goat has been described as the whining baby of the ruminant zodiac. People born under this sign never stop talking and their continuous 'chit chat' sounds like a crying baby. The obvious physical sign of the goat is the goatee, which is a strip of facial fuzz that hangs down like a hairy stalactite. It is seen on men and women of this sign, which can be quite confronting. Goat people have also been known to headbutt stationary objects like walls, fences and tractors. They can do the longest burps of all ruminants with the longest recorded burp timed at 62 seconds.

**BURP VALUE – 7 Bps**

# The Deer 21 June–21 July

Those born in this sign are considered the nicest of all of the ruminants and are known for their physical beauty, big cute eyes and shiny little noses (which can be red). They have a basic intelligence which has evolved into only what is necessary for them to survive. They tend to be trusting of others and willing to burp and let burp. Males born under this sign can be very aggressive to each other when they both like the same girl (doe). To look at one you would never think such a gorgeous creature would burp but don't be deceived, they can belch up to 150 litres of gas a day. The females can be very vain about their appearance.

**BURP VALUE – 7 Bps**

BELCH!

# The Giraffe 21 July–21 August

Those born under this sign are noble, aloof and usually tall! They tend to think that they are above all the other ruminants. That's true because they are taller than them, but it goes a little deeper. These tall ruminants have a different view of the world as they are looking down at everyone else and this colours their personality as markedly as their pretty stripes. They can be rude, arrogant and disinterested in what others have to say. They are always checking their appearance – in fact they will never take a selfie without loads of make-up on! They tend to be very vain and think height is beauty. You will often see females of this sign walking in ridiculously high heels.

**BURP VALUE – 6 Bps**

# The Camel 21 August–21 September

Hump! People born under this sign carry the burden of a water-filled backpack and quite frankly it makes them cranky, short tempered, loud and slightly aggressive. They also have a horribly gross habit – spitting! Yes, they are fond of spitting and will spit directly in your face if you come too close. They are the most odd-looking ruminant in the zodiac. They have pretty frightening green-tinged teeth as well as the most bizarre two-padded marshmallow-like toes. Add up the green teeth, hump, bad temper, spitting and those toes and you definitely get the ruminants' ruminant.

TIP – Approach with caution and never offer your cheek to be kissed.

**BURP VALUE – 8.5 Bps**

# The Buffalo 21 September–21 October

Those born as buffalo are big, in fact they are a member of the BIG 5 (along with elephant, rhino, lion and leopard) but are the only ruminant in the group. They love eating at night, wallowing in mud and hanging out in groups. They are seen to be unpredictable and can go from completely still to becoming a rampaging monster if scared or cornered. They are very protective of their young. If you fall under this sign, you can be quite cliquey. Females all group together and go grass shopping, the young males group together as well. They are blessed with a large head, thick neck, broad chest and strong legs. They are renowned for having one of the smoothest tongues in the ruminant kingdom. They graze widely, eat big and BURP hugeeeeee.

**BURP VALUE – 9 Bps**

# The Moose 21 October–21 November

The moose is also a big ruminant beastie, apparently as blind as a bat but with superb hearing and sense of smell. Those born under this sign can hear whatever you say from 100 metres away, so it's probably wise not to say anything mean about the size of their huge freaky feet! Moose love to swim and compete in water sports. The moose is, as a rule, slow-moving and placid, but if scared it can run like the wind. The moose can belt along up to 60 kilometres per hour, which is great for weekend getaways along country roads. They tend to be tall and have long legs, large nostrils and a big upper lip. Males bellow loudly to get the females' attention. The large nostrils and upper lip are the perfect launch weapons for big bad belches. They also love the smell of a fresh burp, which is handy because they burp a lot. Usually they are very relaxed and good to be around, so if you belong to this sign, people like you a lot.

**BURP VALUE – 8 Bps**

# The Antelope 21 November–21 December

Those born in this sign are athletic, elegant and graceful. They have well-developed molars and a hard upper gum pad. They are the talkers of the zodiac and they bellow, bark, whistle, moo and trumpet to each other. They can be quite arrogant with regards to their appearance and groom frequently, they are very proud of their eyes, which are located on the sides of their heads with a broad field of view. The antelope eats very quickly, their little mouths chomping and chewing small bites, which allows them to sprint away if any danger is sensed. They 'Pronk and Stott' when excited, which is jumping up and down on all four stiff, straight legs. They burp like they eat, frequent little dainty belches that clear their gut gas. Males tend to have three to four girlfriends at any one time. An elegant figure, small features and hoofs as well as lovely coloured skin tones make the antelope a pretty ruminant.

**BURP VALUE – 7 Bps**

# The Yak 21 December–21 January

The yak descended from the cow millions of years ago. They have a thick, shaggy coat of wool all over their body which almost touches the ground. This thick coat insulates them against extreme cold climates, which they experience in their mountain habitat. Those born under this sign love to wear thick, woolly turtleneck jumpers, fluffy jackets and even furry woolly undies. Long hair and beards are favourites of this sign. Yaks have bigger hearts and lungs than their cow cousins at lower altitudes and this is true of all born of this sign. Their large hearts reflect in their generosity, kindness and loyalty. People born under this sign have almost no sweat glands and don't enjoy or thrive in the heat. Scientists say yaks have no detectable odour in their bodily functions – they even have odourless poo! So if you're born under this sign you love to smell perfumed. You enjoy sharing your flatulence and eructation because they have no smell! You tend to eat large quantities but chew slowly, which lengthens the fermentation process.

**BURP VALUE – 7.5 Bps**

## The Llama 21 January–21 February

Llamas are fully domesticated creatures who keep an impeccably clean house, love to socialise and are generally happy just to be alive. They are known for their pretty big eyes and multi-coloured woolly coat. Those born under this sign tend to guard and protect people and other llamas close to them. Males tend to like to be surrounded by groups of females. They are very confident, approachable and curious. Family is very important and their protective nature will always come to the fore. If they are provoked or put in a situation where they feel threatened they will bite, spit, headbutt and neck wrestle, which can lead to kicking and stomping. Unlike their camel cousins they have no external hump, which makes them light on their feet and very surefooted. They eat rather slowly and this of course is an issue for digestion.

They burp and belch and have been known to belch loudly when threatened or when they sense danger. This sign doesn't burp as frequently as its camel and cow cousins, but they can be very, very loud!

**BURP VALUE – 5 Bps**

235

# The Reindeer 21 February–21 March

The most famous reindeer of all time is of course the king of Christmas cheer, that cheeky little red-nosed reindeer Rudolph. Those born under this sign are very athletic, they can swim, run and climb many kilometres in a single day. They love the outdoors and are very social, travelling in very large herds to many locations. Their large hooves or feet are a very distinct physical feature and are used to swim and walk through snow. Eating is a delicate affair and the preference is for small amounts of lean and green moss, twigs and branches. Those born under the reindeer sign are usually very attractive but don't know it, they exude beauty, athleticism and inner peace. They have been known to burp in bouts of up to 20 belches in a row after a long swim. All of their belches are happy burps of joy.

**BURP VALUE – 6.5 Bps**

# RUCTUS RELATIONS

# FAMILY FIZZ

Families are like a colour palette, they come in heaps of colours, shades and combinations. If your family, like many, has three generations that can get together and eat a meal, you will be able to witness the family colour palette first-hand in living colour!

Every family member has a different personality, which is a variation on the personality mix of their parents, whose personality is a mix of their parents or your grandparents, and it just goes back through your genes along the lines of your family tree. What does this have to do with burping, you may well ask? The answer is a lot! Genetics can and do play a major role in physical attributes as well as internal or biological traits. For example, your great grandfather might have been a gifted distance runner, lean with an eight-pack of stomach muscles, which is the new six-pack of stomach muscles, just two more. He also might have had an amazing memory for names, places and facts but you can bet on one genetic hand-me-down, his face and features would have been shared with other members of your past or present family.

Besides facial features, natural abilities and physical

attributes, a predisposition to medical problems can also be passed on. Most conditions are of no consequence, but some can be a ticking medical time bomb. Some of the biological traits or problems that can be passed on include excessive sweating, dribbling, smelly armpits and feet, pimples, oily hair, dandruff, flatulence and of course burping!

In this chapter we are dealing with burping and belching in the family. It's sure to be a GAS!

# GASSY GRANDPARENTS

They say getting old is terrible – sore bones, wrinkled skin, false teeth, thinning hair, loss of hearing, loss of vision, loss of memory, loss of mobility, loss of bladder control, the list goes on and that's a lot of losses. Older people can also experience loss of embarrassment and this is observed, or should I say smelled or heard, in their complete disregard for hiding bodily functions. They will fart or burp anywhere, anytime in front of anyone. Burping for grandparents seems to be a very normal, shared, loud family ritual. Your popping pop will blow out a belch and say nothing, like it is his right. He acts like nobody noticed that he just burped out half of the contents of his gut. Your lovely sweet grandmother will burp and belch after every dainty mouthful of everything that she eats or drinks. This will be immediately followed by her saying, 'Ooh, I've got gas today.' The truth is she has gas every day! So just accept that your gassy grandparents burp and belch without control and have a little giggle to yourself because if you are lucky you too will grow old and gassy.

# MARVELLOUS MUMS

Mums have an amazing way of playing everything down and making it all ok. She will lick her finger and wipe off that wart-like little crumb stuck to the side of your mouth without a second thought. If you vomit, Mum will get a washer and wash your mush and make it all new again. Mums don't fear any bodily function, they seem to ignore the most disgusting smells a human can manufacture. They will hold, grasp, rub and wipe every type of yucky substance that their children make without flinching or gagging, which is really quite incredible considering some babies produce smelly nappies that could bring down entire armies. Mums accept burping from their babies as a normal part of life (they even encourage babies to burp!), as well as projectile vomit, diarrhoea and dribble. Mums burp but never belch. They burp as discreetly as possible and usually on the move. Your mum will rarely burp in front of you unless it just sneaks out, in which case she will always say, 'Excuse me!' Burping for mums is framed in good manners, but if she lets one loose she might have a little giggle as well. Mums can do anything and burping is no different.

# DANGEROUS GAS DADDYS

We all know that dads seem to be very relaxed about unleashing gas from either end. Often they seem to do it just to get a reaction and annoy your marvellous mum.

How many times have you heard your father walk through the house and blast out a super beast belch, followed by your mother telling him off for being a pig, at which point he has a chuckle to himself?

Everyone in your household knows that daddy dear is a burping, belching, farting machine with no intention of trying to disguise or hide his bodily functions. He is proud of all of them, but proudest of his gut gas beastie burps, because he knows that they are not as offensive to most people as flatulence, as well as being an important part of the daddy bonding ritual. When his daddy friends assemble at the sacred burping grounds (the BBQ), his daddy pack posse burp and belch with such freedom and enthusiasm you can almost feel the ground rumble and shake.

# BURPING BROTHERS

Remember, younger brothers are gassy fathers in training!
Brothers can be grotty, icky, sticky and smelly at the best
of times, so burping is as normal as breathing to them.
They will burp anywhere, anytime and do it frequently
to annoy or tease people. Young brothers practise and
experiment with their burps and belches. They try to
produce them, manipulate them and even create new
ones. The little brother is the burping research scientist,
even though he has no formal knowledge of belching. His
talent lies in his ability to produce so many burps. He will
always drink carbonated drinks to fuel his burp research.
He is a trailblazer, taking burps where they have never
gone before, but mostly into the faces of his little sister,
pets and fellow burping friends.

# SPARKLING SISTERS

Sisters love to burp and giggle and belch and chuckle
when they are with their BFFP – Best Friends Forever
Posse. They are also often observed slurping fizzy
carbonated drinks whilst having dancing burp

competitions. Busting moves and burping are common pastimes seen in rumpus rooms all over the world at any given time. But, if you place your sister anywhere near boys, you will never ever hear the faintest hint of a burp. In public your sister has absolutely NO bodily functions – no burps, no belches, no farts, no anything! The theory is that your sister doesn't want anyone to know that she has any bodily functions except for her BFFP. Well, that's the theory, but we all know that sisters can burp and belch with the biggest and baddest gut gas explosions. For now though, we will all pretend that your sisters never make any loud fizzy bubbly belches.

# AERATED AUNTIES

Aunties always breeze in when they visit bearing a swag full of gifts for all. They always appear to be as happy as a gaggle of teenage girls at a One Direction concert. Aunties have an air of mystery about them, air being the operative word. They are usually beautifully dressed, smelling of citrus and frangipani and seem to glide around the house like they are floating on rollerskates. Aunties laugh and chuckle a lot, more than most family members. You have probably noticed that when your aunty visits, lots of eating, drinking and chatting takes place, usually around the kitchen bench, and this is where you can spot your aunty letting out sneaky little burps.

Aunties talk a lot and they do it very quickly which makes them swallow lots of air. Add fizzy drinks and excitement and aunty is fuelled up and ready to get her burp on. If you watch her closely she will chat and often raise her hand over her mouth like she is wiping her cheek. She uses this distraction to pop out a few little baby belches. Her favourite distraction is the Napkin Wipe 'n' Burp. She will go to wipe her mouth with a napkin and as she pretends to wipe you can bet your belching aunty's rollerskates that she is burping under that cloth.

# BUBBA WUBBA BURPING BABIES

Babies are cute, just about everyone thinks so, but we all know they leak lots of gas, vomit and poop. In fact, some regard the human baby as a 'gas-vomit-poo machine' because besides crying and sleeping that is all they do. We are focussing on the burping bubba and it's quite interesting why babies are burped. Babies can get a build-up of gas in their stomachs because they often lay in one position for many hours, which stops movements that help expel the gas. Parents are advised to burp bubba directly after feeding. This is advisable because if it isn't done the baby can wake up hours later screaming due to the build-up of gas! Burping bubba is a safe and satisfying way to keep him or her gas free. Babies can be very uncomfortable when gas builds up from swallowing air, crying and drinking milk. If the gas is not released it can cause lots of pain.

Bubba is not only given training to burp, but is encouraged to belch on cue after drinking milk. Burping a baby is done by gently patting its back until the gas starts to be belched up. Babies swallow lots of air when they cry and scream, but crying and screaming for extended periods can also indicate that bubba has developed colic, which is the build-up of gas in the gut and intestine. Bubba Must Burp, full stop!

# A BURP BY ANY OTHER NAME

# ALL THE BURP NAMES

It's always good to expand your vocabulary. Here are some names for the burp that you might not know.
Belch,

Burp,

Blast,

Blurp,

B-Lurp,

Bloof,

Bloomf,

Gut Blast,

Belch Blast,

Gut Trumpet,

Barking Rat,

Bean Blurp,

Baked Blast,

Bean Bomb,

Bean Bang,

Raucous Ructus,

Blampf,

Bork,

Gut Bubble,

Bongo,

    Cheek Squeak,

        Word Bomb,

            Crunchy Frog,

                Flutter-blast,

                    Duck Call,

                        Dog Bark,

                        Bung,

                  Throat Frog,

              Croak-a-Cola,

            Gut Biscuit,

        Gas Guzzle,

    Gas Groan,

      Gas Mass,

          Gut Gronk,

             Gas Gush,

                Gut Frog,

                    Tree Frog,

                      Eruction,

Ructus,

Ramburpious,

Bobby Belch,

Burp Bump,

Blurrrr,

Borrrrk,

Gas Grunt,

Burp-Gular,

Mouth Fart,

Fizz-a-Saurus,

Burpasaurus,

Brr Brr,

Eruptive Eructation.

# GAS GLOSSARY

See below for a list of my favourite burping words! If you can think of a burp word that is not in this list (or you invent a new one!), email me your word at **burptionary@gmail.com**

**Belch** to emit wind noisily from the stomach through to the mouth explosively with force. To belch out an offensively loud and smelly belly volcano.

**Belchograph** a photo of a burp in motion. Very rare.

**Burp** when gas is released from the stomach via the mouth, usually accompanied by a percussive sound and a slight to excessive stink.

**Burp-a-cise** a type of exercise that is done to funky music and involves lots of burping and krumping.

**Burpaholic** a person who is addicted to burping – they burp anywhere, anytime in front of anyone.

**Burpaliscious** the incredibly rank residue left in the mouth after a burptacular event.

**Burpasaurus** a prehistoric king of the dinosaurs, it used to paralyse its prey by burping directly into its victim's face, thus stunning it and making it fall and roll over.

**Burptionality** the country in which a burp is born.

**Burpionarian** a librarian with a special interest in burps.

**Burpocrisy** when a person says they think burping in public is disgusting, but then they do it all the time.

**Burpologist** a specialist who studies burping and belching and is a true master of the art form.

**Burpology** the scientific study of burps and belching.

**Burpometrist** a person who studies the effects of burping on eyesight.

**Burponics** a branch of science and technology that deals with burps and electricity.

**Burpopolis** an ancient city where people worshipped the burp and the belch. Often at war with Fartopolis.

**Burptacular** the loudest, most amazing, sensational, percussive, stenchy, explosive burp. A word used to describe something unbelievably great.

**Burptastic** similar to burptacular but a little more fantastic.

**Burptionary** a factual funny book about everything to do with burping written by a genius who is also hilarious.

**Burptopia** a fictional place where the burp has replaced the spoken word.

**Burpy-lingual** someone who can speak burp and belch fluently.

**Digestion** the process in which food is converted into substances that are absorbed by the body.

**Eructation** the voiding of gas or acidic fluid from the stomach to the mouth.

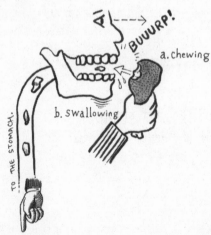

**Expel** to force something out.

**Gas** an air-like substance which expands freely to fill any available space.

**Gob** slang word for your mouth – that small round multi-purpose opening in the middle of your face used for breathing, talking, belching, burping, dribbling, singing, spitting, drooling, eating, drinking, whistling, screaming, kissing, blowing raspberries, vomiting, smiling and laughing to name a few things you do with your gob.

**Gut** another name for your stomach or belly.

**Oesophagus** the muscular membranous tube for the passage of food from the pharynx (throat) to the stomach.

**Peristalsis** wave-like muscular contractions that aid in digestion of food from the mouth to the bottom.

**Ructus** another word for belching.

**Slurpy burpy** a wet, sloppy burp, sometimes produced after sucking on a slurpee.

# About the author

ANDY JONES appeared in a plume of gas. They say the gas was rainbow-coloured and had flashing lights, not unlike a disco. Andy, being the shrewd improviser he is, put this chemical phenomenon to good use and built 3 shows around it: 'What's the Joke', 'Electric Music' and 'Kamokidz', which he has been touring all over Australia and New Zealand at school halls, libraries and festivals full of fun-loving, funky kids.

Andy also realised that he had a passion for all body functions and has devoted his life to unravelling the slimy, sticky and sometimes smelly mystery of their why, where and how! Andy has taken burp gas where it has never been – to the stages and classrooms of Australia. So get ready to boogie in Andy's disco gas plume in a school or library near you.

Burp on!

## About the illustrator

DAVID PUCKERIDGE may well be an illustrator but he is also a master burper. He has entered the World Burping Championships numerous times and has his sphincter set on dethroning Tim Janus.

David's ability to illustrate something you can't even see is truly remarkable. His work in *The Fartionary* is a visual masterpiece.

He has illustrated several books, including *Hello Burp, Pleased to Smell You, The Gassy Wizard* and *Are you There Burp? It's Me, David.*\*

\* Some or all of the above may not be the exact 100% truth!

## Also by Andy Jones

The Enormous Book of Hot Jokes for Kool Kids

The Fartionary

The Adventures of Scooterboy & Skatergirl

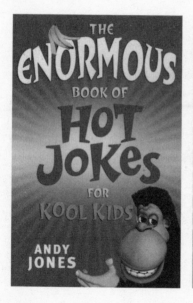 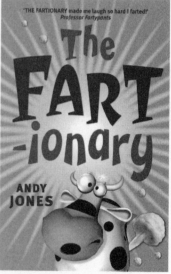